A VAMPIRE'S TREASURE

FATE'S CHRONICLES SERIES
BOOK II

RHIANNON FUTCH

CONTENTS

The living room seems much smaller with Natasha and Billy in it together. I don't know how this will work, but we have to give it a try. The two of them spend all their time here as it is, and they cannot keep falling asleep in random places. It mortified me when I found Billy asleep in a tub in one of the bathrooms, after I had used the facilities. This just can't go on and they are going to have to see that, whether or not they like it. I look to Devon for encouragement, all he has for me is raised eyebrows and determination.

Billy and Natasha glare at each other from their chairs on the other side of the table. Deep breath, you can do this. "Hey! Can you stop with the glaring at each other? I begin to think you two are doing this just to flirt with each other." Matching gasps of outrage emerge from Billy and Natasha making me laugh, "I really do need to talk to you both. Without all the attitude for five minutes." The two nod their agreement, forced as it is. Continuing on I say, "After the recent bathtub debacle and other incidents," Billy and Natasha both light up in blushes, "Devon and I have decided that we need to do things a different way for the time being. We think that all the work we are doing would benefit by having the two of you living here." They begin a chorus of the reasons why they could never live in the same house together. They are loud and I can't deal with that today so I create a barrier of air around them, effectively cutting them off from bombarding us with the noise. Devon chuckles while we wait for the two of them to subside and be ready to talk about this like adults. Natasha is the first to notice and cuts off her rant, crossing her arms in front of her and giving me a hard glare. Waving a hand, I remove hers and leave Billy's in place as he is still going on his tangent. Natasha tells me, "That was a dirty trick."

"Yes, it was. I just can't with the yelling today and so I pulled a dirty trick. Are you ready to talk reasonably about this or would you rather yell into the void a bit more?"

Rolling her eyes at me, Natasha says, "Fine. Yes, I am willing to talk reasonably. I don't want to give up my apartment. I love that place. I don't want to live in such close proximity to the yelling oaf over there that hasn't even realized he isn't being heard by anyone but himself."

Smiling as I watch Billy realize we are talking but he can't hear us, I tell Natasha, "I wouldn't ask you to give up your apartment." Billy is quiet now so I wave my hand to let him in on the conversation, "You should keep your apartment, I wouldn't want you to let that go. But, you could have a room and things here so that you have a place to sleep that isn't the floor of a random room. The same goes for you, Billy. No one should be sleeping in bathtubs. It's just creepy. The both of you spend the majority of your time here, there is no reason why you shouldn't have your own bedrooms. Natasha, you especially. You are my right hand and I need you near me to help in sorting through all of this. Between the business, my new duties as Chronicler, the mess with Charles, and all the things left over from Charlie… That is a lot for any one witch. I need you. Devon needs you Billy, and to some extent so do I." Natasha and Billy are looking very serious now, but they appear to be thinking it over. That is more than I had hoped for so soon into this conversation. Billy speaks first, "Aye, you might be right. It certainly wasn't the most comfortable thing to wake up and realize that someone was a using the loo on the other side of the shower curtain. We manage to avoid each other most of the time, should be easier when we sleep. I'll do it. I don' want a room right next to her though! She probably snores." He grins briefly, a flash of white in the ebony planes of his face. Natasha narrows her eyes at him, "I think a room will be fine for now, wherever is fine. Decent sleep would be nice too."

I am stunned that the two of them have become so reasonable and so quickly, but I will not look this gift horse in the butt. "Great! That's settled, how about you and I go find you a bedroom after we get done here Natasha?" She nods her agreement and I move on to the next item, "Now, about the business. I have been thinking about this. I want it to be a helping organization, charitable one. Unfortunately, that will eventually mean fundraising. But I think we can do the magical community a lot of good and mostly right out in the open." Natasha's eyes have lit up, and she is leaning forward in her chair, "Fate, I love it! Can we do fundraising galas? I have always wanted to put together a gala!" Laughing, I nod, "Of course. We need reasons to wear glorious dresses. I was thinking we could do shows for sick kids, make them magical right out in the open. Everyone will believe it is part of the show and the kids will love it. We could have advocates for children, but maybe with a focus on the magic ones. I would like to believe that all of the magical community will be good to their children, but we know they aren't all good. We could connect the ones they label as problems because of their abilities with counselors familiar with the magical world." Billy is near bouncing with excitement as he says, "What about setting up a foster network? We could act as an agency for connecting problem children with fosters specializing in those kinds of problems. We could offer," he holds up his fingers in air quotes, "trainings. I actually know some people that have a bit of experience with the foster system. I have been working at getting in touch with them recently for other reasons, but they could be a big help in getting this set up. Just based on the experience they have with fostering kids from the magical community."

"Oh Holy Hera, that would be perfect! Yes! Get in touch with them and ask whether they would be willing to take part in getting this set up. I would love to talk to them if they aren't able to travel here for whatever reason."

Natasha chimes in, "What are we going to call it though? And where will we base it? I know we have been working from here, but that won't be a viable set up for long."

"You are so right," Devon says, "that is why we have asked Maggie to set up touring some available buildings that might be appropriate for Fate's purposes. If you two could work together, then finding the building would likely go much faster." Both Billy and Natasha roll their eyes at him and turn back to focus on me, "I don't know yet what we will call it. We can brainstorm on that this week. In that same vein, I have to start going through these spells that have been collected and left for safekeeping with Devon. I need to begin my duties as Chronicler and I plan to devote a couple hours daily to that end. It sure would help if I was a vampire and didn't need sleep as often as I do now." I look hard at Devon, who squirms in his seat.

"I feel like you should consider this more thoroughly before you jump into things. Besides, being newly turned is a lot to deal with all by itself." Billy's face says Devon is skirting the truth, and the fear I feel from the bond between us speaks to a different reason for the stall. He must not want to talk about it in front of Natasha and Billy, so I let it go. For now.

"Still, Natasha, I think we can get through a lot of these spells and weed out duplicates, add in variations, and in general update the entire book."

"I think that is a good plan. Grams said we can definitely add her spell to the book. She feels honored to be included. Apparently she knew about it, but wasn't one of the original families that started the books."

"Oh. Well, that is fascinating. Hmm, I wonder why she didn't share the information with you before now?"

Natasha shrugs, "No idea. Maybe she had a feeling she needed to keep it to herself until now."

Altering space in a building is surprisingly easy. My office wasn't quite big enough to do all I need to be able to do in there, with the setting up of my foundation, duties as Chronicler, and all the research I need to do. Half of it is dedicated to craft and anyone not a part of the magical community that enters the office will not be able to see that half as it would only confuse them. I have a nice lectern situated on that side to hold whatever tome I am researching currently. The work tables I scavenged from thrift stores since I was fully aware that I would be scarring them up anyway. My desk still sits in the same place, but now there is a shiny new filing cabinet nearby. The window is much larger and lets in so much light; I love it.

I have a couple bookshelves on the other side as well, there are a couple of grimoires that branches of the families turned over for lack of heirs to hand it down to. Plus the one that I am Chronicling in, it is huge. Though from what I understand it won't seem any bigger. However, I feel I may need to spell it eventually to control the weight of the book. The space it takes up may have been altered already, but the weight of the book was not included in that alteration. I don't imagine anyone could have guessed it would be tasked with holding so much information.

It amazed Natasha when she saw it the first time. She couldn't believe how big a book it is. Now we are working our way through it and the spells not already contained within the book, and we are equally amazed at all the overlap. So many spells to have a child. Even more to heal a sick child. The time of measles pandemics was horrible, and the Spanish flu even worse. I can't imagine how many witches over spent their energies healing as many as they could.

For now, I am perusing the book while I wait for Natasha to arrive. She left for her apartment this morning for clothing and such to keep here. She texted about 20 minutes ago saying she was on her way. She is probably putting her things away in her room. I am taking notes as I go through the book, on similar spells and which families created them.

I hear my phone beep on the desk and turn to go get it. I see Natasha standing on the other side of the room, looking very annoyed. She and Billy must have passed each other in the hall.

"Hey, what kept you? Why do you look so annoyed?" I ask her as I pick up my phone. Checking the message, I see it is from Natasha. I look over at her, "Why did you text me when you were here?"

She rolls her eyes at me, "I have been here for the past twenty minutes! I couldn't get in and you couldn't hear me! I sent the message to your phone in the hope that the noise from it would penetrate this thing."

My mouth forms an O as I look between her and the thin glimmer that is the boundary between the two halves of the room. "I had no idea. Can you go in now?"

I watch as she puts her hand through the barrier first, followed by the rest of her. "Can you still hear me?"

Natasha nods and says, "Yes."

I step up to the boundary and put my hand through no problem. I step fully into the area and shrug at Natasha, "Maybe it is because I made it?"

Sighing, Natasha asks, "Did you put in the spell that it was to allow magical people that live here to enter freely?"

"Um, no. That didn't occur to me…" This blushing thing sucks. "Sorry. I can cast it again and add that."

Natasha shakes her head no, "I think you should leave it as is. Call Devon. See if he and Billy can walk in while I am in here."

"Ok, this might be fun to watch." I message the two of them as I say, "So you could see that I was in here, you just couldn't get through or get me to hear you?"

"Right."

Billy walks in first and straight toward us. He gets to the barrier, first hitting it with his toes, slamming his knee into it and then stopping himself from hitting the barrier with his face by throwing his hands up to break his fall. Natasha starts laughing and while we can't hear what Billy is saying, I don't think it is complimentary. Devon walks in and his jaw drops, Billy must be really cursing up a storm out there. He looks over at us and grins. Billy seems to be starting a whole new rant as Devon walks over and puts his hand against the barrier. I step up to the barrier and touch my hand to his, our fingers entwine and he steps through the barrier into my arms. He feels so nice. Turning his upper body, he puts a hand through the barrier. Billy walks over, takes his hand and steps through. He gives me such a look saying, "You could have at least warned me."

Grinning, I ask, "Where is the fun in that? Besides, you would have done the same. Now, one more test. If I leave this side, can you all depart as you will? Or are you trapped until I return?"

Devon releases me, and I step around him, out of the barrier. He puts his hand against the barrier and pushes right through to stand at my side. Billy and Natasha are another story, they try the same and nothing happens. But we can hear them from our side of the barrier. It is a most curious thing, Devon and I step back through.

I say, "Well, I do not understand how this happened, but I think I should work out the details to fix it for the three of you at the very least. I need you all to be able to come in here should anything happen to me."

Devon growls, "Nothing is going to happen to you this time. I am going to make sure of it. No matter what. If I have to end Charles, then so be it." He crushes me a little in this big hug and I tell him, "While I like the way you think, it is still a possibility. Charles could get to me. The killer my husband hired before he died could sniper me through a window. I could get in a car wreck and die. Cancer. Heart attack. Lightening could strike. Until I am turned, I am pretty easy to kill and my chances of dying are the same as anyone else. You have to accept that if you aren't going to turn me anytime soon."

Devon groans and squeezes me tight again, "I don't want to lose you, but that is a risk I have to take for now." He lets go and puts his hands on my shoulders, "Please, just be cautious? For me?"

"Of course. I am not in any hurry to die now that I am loving my life so much. Still though, it would be one less worry if you turned me."

Natasha chimes in, "I agree. Of all of us, she is the most at risk. Turning her would alleviate a lot of that risk. For now, though, she and I have work to do. Scram, both of you. Fate and I don't need supervision."

Billy shrugs and strolls on out, if carefully. Devon gives me one last kiss before he too walks out.

Turning to Natasha, I ask her, "Are you ready to cast the recognition spell on me now?"

"Yes, let's get it done and then we can work on this. Do you want to put it in the book first or after?"

"After. I think I can describe it better if I watch you cast it. Did your grandmother cast it on you?"

"Yeah, she said with the way I go through guys I needed to be able to recognize a snake in the grass if one found me. She said she never bothered with mom though, mom never looked at guys much till she met dad and after she met him she was done. No other guy ever caught her attention again. Since it seemed mutual Grams didn't see the point."

I continued to pepper her with questions as she readied the elements of the spell. Everything in place she begins and I fall silent, just feeling the magic build and watching as she moves through the ritual. Natasha is all grace and beauty as she walks around me in her bare feet, with jeans and today's garnet colored silk shirt. I could watch her cast spells for days. Her hair is unbound, and it floats a little like flames when she uses her magic. I feel the spell settle over me like a blanket of love and soak in. My third eye lights up and opens more than it has ever done. I am surprised by this, but I will record it in the book. Natasha is watching me expectantly, so I ask, "Does everyone get the weird feeling in their third eye after this?"

She frowns, "Some do. Most feel a warm blanket settling on them and then they just know. Grams told me the ones that feel the weirdness in their third eye had the ability already, they just needed to open to it."

"Oh."

"Yeah. It's a little weird for you to have that. Think Pru will let us cast it on her? I want to know if she has it too or is that a soul thing."

"I don't know. Let me message her and see if she will come over?" I send a quick text to Pru, asking if she has time to come over. She immediately texts back, saying she has time, and she needs the address. I send that and she says she will see me in twenty. "Ok, she is coming over. Let's get this spell recorded while we wait. Oh, I need to text Billy. He is playing doorman today." I send the text to Billy and the two of us get to work on a fresh page in the book. As we finish recording her grandmother's spell in the book Natasha takes a picture to send to her grandmother.

"Grams wanted a picture?"

"She didn't ask, no. But she was very honored to be asked for one of her spells to go in the book. She said only the most powerful or most popular of witches, the ones with the right connections, were asked to be part of the Chronicle. She said she always thought that was such a shame."

"I think I know why, but did she say what her reason was?"

"Of course she did. She loves to tell me her reasons. She says that it might educate me the way my mother never did. She said that by keeping it restricted to those particular families they cut off a world of knowledge. So many other families with their long lineages quietly going about their business and we miss out on saving their knowledge because they don't have the right last name."

"I thought as much. Well, I do not have any reservations about adding spells from all witches that would like to. We can start more books if we need to. There is no reason to not include the other witches. I mean, my family wasn't included either, but they are now."

"Oh good. Grams said if that was how you responded that I could tell you the rest."

"The rest? There's more? What?"

"Oh, there is definitely more. Grams has been collecting grimoires. As did her mother and her mother before her. Anytime a family died out or didn't have an heir in their direct line, they passed their books on to them. So Grams said if you responded right, you get the grimoires. All the grimoires she has and there are about a hundred."

My jaw drops, "A hundred? Are you joking? Holy Hera, that is a lot! Why wouldn't they be included? This is bananas. When does she want us to come collect them? I mean, that is going to take a long time to get catalogued and added, we are going to need help. I need to hire someone else. I wonder if Maggie could recommend someone? Ugh. I still have to do the other interviews. I need to put her on retainer."

Natasha laughs, "You should put her on retainer. And you should hire another person to help with this. It doesn't matter whether or not they are a witch, but they have to be lovers of knowledge for the sake of knowledge. Bookworm for sure, maybe a librarian type? Not like us, we were never the kind of librarian I am talking about. I mean the kind that dreams about being a librarian from the time they find out what a library is."

About that time I see Pru walk in and narrow her eyes at the barrier. I quickly step over and put my hand thru, she takes it and walks in. "Why, sister, why do you have a barrier like this in your office? Oh, I see, you didn't think the spell all the way thru." I drop her hand like a hot potato. I hate it when she reads me like that. Pru smirks at me and wanders over to hug Natasha. I feel research for another spell coming on, and this one is not going to be one Pru likes. She is so polite to everyone else, but she seems to think access to my inner thoughts is her right. I hate it.

"Pru, while it is always lovely to have you in my head uninvited, we asked you here for a different reason."

"I saw. And yes, you can cast the spell on me. I want to know too. I think I can gauge pretty accurately whether or not what I feel is the same as what you felt since I got to see/feel it in your head."

I narrow my eyes at her for that last remark. She knows how invasive I feel her stepping into my mind is and the ethics around doing it. Why does she do it to me? Going to find myself a spell to stop that shit. I watch as Natasha sets up to do the spell again, but my mind wanders. Perhaps there will be a spell in the archive to accomplish keeping her out of my head without having to throw up shields every time I see her, touch her, am in the same house with her. I wonder what else she lifts out of my head when she does that? I am so done with this nonsense...

"It isn't the same."

I jump hearing Pru speak, "Pardon?"

She glares at me, "I said, it isn't the same. What you felt and what happened to me were totally different animals. I felt the warm blanket feeling. You got that, but then it all went to your third eye."

I look over at Natasha, "I guess that answers the question. It is not a family thing at all, this particular talent is soul-linked. Do you think it could be linked to the number of incarnations? Like once you have incarnated 5 times as a witch, this is the door prize?"

Natasha was very attentive to what I was saying right up to the end, that was when she lost it. Laughter bubbled up out of her like lava out of a child's volcano project. Pru and I both joined in, her laughter can be infectious. We all manage to calm ourselves eventually and Natasha says, "I don't think it is exactly a door prize, more like something your soul has developed over time."

Pru shakes her head, "Well then, why haven't I or you developed the same thing?"

"We didn't need to be able to recognize them Pru," Natasha tells her as gently as possible. "We didn't have a hundreds of years old vampire looking to kill us every time we incarnate on this planet."

"So my third eye might have woken up on its own within the next few weeks anyway?" I am floored with the implications. What if this ability woke up every time Charles began trying to kill me? How wild is that? How many other creatures did he use trying to make me dead?

Pru shrugs, "Well, whatever. I need to go practice recognizing others in the magical community. Say, can you remove this if I decide I hate it?"

Natasha answers, "Yes. You don't even have to be here for us to do it. So just let us know."

Pru nods, "I suppose that will have to do. I am off. The mall is probably a good place to find the magical community, right?"

"As good as anywhere else." I reply, quickly throwing up all my shields as she comes in for a hug. She smirks again when she feels my shields and gives them a good smack. It hurts, but I hold them firm anyway, glaring at her. I wait until she is out the door to text Billy to let me know when she is out. He sends back a head-scratch emoji and an ok. A few minutes later, I get the text from him. Natasha has waited patiently the entire time, I love her so much. "Now that Pru is all the way out of the building, we can get to work. Today we are after two things, combining double spell entries and finding a spell to block mind-readers."

Natasha lifts an eyebrow, "Care to elaborate?"

I tell her the whole thing about how Pru is constantly invading my head and using it against me. How I hate it and throw up shields when I remember, how she loves to thump those shields, and how it hurts like hell every time she thumps them. Natasha is proper horrified, "She has never done that… Wait. Has she been invading all of us and just kept it quiet all this time? Girl, this is not cool. We need to find that spell now. I got too many dirty things in my head that are not meant to be shared." We move to stand in front of the podium, Natasha pulls her laptop over to record the titles of the spells and what they do while I go through pages.

LET THE HUNT BEGIN.

❧ 3 ☙

It has been three days since we started looking for the spell to keep Pru out of our heads. I didn't want to see her so when she messaged that she wanted to come by I told her I was on my way out for the day on business. It wasn't true then, but I made it so.

Natasha called her Grams and asked if we could come by and pick her brain for a possible spell, it thrilled her to have us over. I pull into the little driveway at Natasha's Gram's house; it is just the same as when we were younger. Overgrown everywhere in the best way with loads of herbs and witching plants. The little bungalow nestles in like it had never been any other way. It feels good just stepping out of the car and into the energy of the place. Like nothing bad could ever happen so long as you were here, in this place. I see Natasha soaking it all in just the way I am, this sense of wellbeing is like mana for our busy souls.

I see the door open and we both shut our car doors, beginning the walk up the path to her home. Griselda smiles wide as she watches us walk up, "I have missed your faces, I have. It is too long between visits! You must come by more often. I think I will dole out the books one per visit so you will come see me every time you want another." She cackles at her statement, I am pretty sure she isn't joking at all but I don't mind the excuse to come see her and she knows it. We reach her and hug, one great group hug. She is the best person to hug, she radiates balance. Hug done, she shoos us inside and along to the kitchen at the back of the house. There is a book sitting on the table, but so is tea. And cookies.

We sit and she pours for us, into her delicate china cups, placing three cookies on each saucer. Passing them out she asks, "Now, why are you searching for this one in particular?"

Natasha takes the lead, explaining our reasons. I appreciate that because it is embarrassing to be magically bullied by my own kid sister like this. I feel Grams watching me with her keen eyes; I bring mine up to meet hers. She reaches across the table and takes my hand, sympathy written in the lines of her face.

"Oh sweet girl, you shouldn't have borne that all alone so long. Here is something your parents didn't want you to know, but that your sister does know, you were adopted by them. They told your sister when you were both young, as soon as her gifts began to develop." She shakes her head, "You see, they didn't think they could have children. So they spent time looking for a magical child. I think most hid their talents for fear of exploitation. But you sparkled like the stars, even to them. Your mother always swore that your magic allowed her to get pregnant, since she was pregnant within months of adopting you. Suspicion grew in the two of them after that, so when your sister developed the talent to read minds they set her to monitor you." My mouth hangs open, my eyes wide as I try to process all of this. Why wouldn't they tell me I was adopted? What suspicions? They made Pru like this?

I croak out the one question burning thru my mind, "Why?" Natasha scoots her chair over and throws an arm around me. I lean in for the comfort.

Grams continues, "I need to tell you the whole sorry mess. It isn't pretty, but I helped you where I could. It is why you have always been so dear to me, I consider you one of my own. Who knows, maybe you are related in some way? I stray, your parents. Your parents became very paranoid, and they brought you over to consult with me. They wanted to know if there was a way to keep you from using your powers, they were worried you would hurt your baby sister, they said."

"I would never!"

She holds up a hand, "I know you wouldn't. You don't have it in you. They said you got annoyed at her crying once and demanded they sing to the baby because you didn't know the songs. As soon as they began to sing she quieted and they decided you were too powerful and too wild, you must be restrained. I told them it wasn't possible, and I spread the word throughout the community that no one was to aid them in this quest of theirs. They tried various practitioners, but the word spread far beyond our community. Once Prudence developed her abilities, they saw that as an answer to their problems. They had her spy on your innermost thoughts and report to them. They were positively awful to Prudence quite often because she didn't tell them what they wanted to hear. She began to lie to them, even as they taught her that it was her duty to police the thoughts of others. To cast aside ethics in the pursuit of information. It has made her a suspicious witch that uses her abilities with no regard for the ethics of her actions." Grams pauses to sip her tea, grimacing when it is cold and holding it out to Natasha who obliges her by heating it up. She sips again, this time with a sigh of contentment. "I felt like this would be the reason that you were seeking this spell. So, I will give you two. The first is the spell you seek, a way to armor yourself against anyone invading your thoughts. The second is a spell of binding. The one your parents sought. Once you are all protected from your sister invading your thoughts, you will feel her attempting, it will no longer hurt but you will feel a strange sensation crawling over your skin. If your sister will not abide by ethical practices, it will be up to you to stop her."

"Oh no, no, please. I don't, I don't want this responsibility. Can't someone else take this on?"

"No child. It is for you to do, because you will do it from a place of love. Whereas I could not because while I pity your sister, I just don't like her."

"I don't want this Grams. I don't want it at all. But I see what you are saying and I will, if there is no other way. I have a question, maybe you can answer it, do you know where I came from originally? Where they adopted me from at least?"

"I can tell you some of that. They said they adopted you out of Armenia. The orphanage said you were placed in the lap of one of the few nuns in Armenia by God. The nun said there was a bright light and then you were laying across her lap, she heard a voice say take care of my baby. They never found out anything more from the nun and no relatives ever came forward. Your parents said that in your record it listed you as a child of God. Perhaps you could do the DNA things? To find your people? Oh, and they wanted you to look like them. I think the time has come to drop that spell, unless you would prefer to stay hidden as you are?"

"What? What do you mean, hidden as I am?"

"I mean your parents cast a strong glamour on you as a baby. Natasha, I am surprised you never saw it. Your education was lacking, girl!"

Natasha pulls back and squints her eyes as she studies me, "I see it! Holy shit girl, what DO you look like?"

"Well, when she was a baby, she was darker. I imagine it is much the same now. She probably looks similar to you, Natasha, but with her own facial features. I don't think they changed those."

I know my eyes must be like saucers at this point. I don't even know what to do with all this. I pull my phone out of my back pocket and turn on the camera. I snap a quick selfie, then look back at Grams as I set the phone down. The picture showed me as I look right now, plain white Jane, shell-shocked but otherwise very normal. "Yes, I want it dropped. How long will it take you to get ready?"

Grams laughs and waves her hand at me. I feel a tingle start at the top of my head and travel slowly down my body as Grams says, "Some things don't need preparation."

I watch Natasha as the feeling progresses down my face and neck, her eyes are huge and her mouth is hanging open, "Girl, you could be my sister. That hair is gorgeous. Why would they hide this?"

I wait impatiently for the tingling to stop before I pick up my phone. I hand it over to Natasha, "Take a picture, I can't do it." She takes the phone and flips the camera out of selfie mode. All too quickly, I hear the click. She touches the screen and hands the phone back to me. I close my eyes and turn the phone toward me. Peeking through the smallest of slits, I see brown skin and jet hair in the picture. I open my eyes a little wider, a little more. I could be Natasha's sister. Holy Hera, why did they hide this? I send the picture to Devon. He immediately sends back a question mark. I write back, *My parents glamoured me when I was a baby. Nat's Grammy Griselda just got rid of it. Think you can deal with a brown-skinned woman?*

It was always about the soul babe. You have the most beautiful soul I have ever encountered. The new packaging is just as attractive as the prior.

I press the phone to my chest, tears leaking down my face. Natasha asks, "What did he say? Do I need to kick his balls up to his chin?" She grabs the phone from me and reads the last text, "Oh hell girl. That's the sweetest thing I have ever seen a man write. Grams," she passes the phone over, "look at this."

Her eyes get a little misty, "Ah, he is as sweet and smooth as my Fernando was when he lived."

I clear my throat to regain use of my voice, "He is very sweet. This is why I chose him so long ago. But Grams, we have been here much too long. We do actually have business to work on and I think I need some different clothing. I bought all my stuff with pale skin in mind…"

Grams gets up, "Take this book, it has both spells within it. You record all the spells, use the one and keep the other handy. You can unbind her, if she truly changes. That one is in the book as well. Now get going, both of you. I want to see you again soon!"

Natasha and I both hug her goodbye, she feels so frail these days. I think all the books that weren't included will have their own separate chronicle. I need to write the vampire stuff down too. This whole crazy story of ours has to be part of a chronicle, because people are going to want to hear the story one day and I am only telling it once. Stepping out of her house and back into the bright light of day is harsh on the eyes. Our walk back to the car is leisurely, with stops to smell the plants.

Back in the car again, we head directly to our favorite little café. The traffic is not terrible and we arrive in reasonable time. Natasha and I luck out with table outside after we order. We immediately delve into the situation of my new look.

"You could borrow some of my clothes until you get your own... Not that... Those clothes are really awful on the new you." Natasha finally gets her entire issue out and I am relieved she isn't going to let me down gently.

"I agree—" Our food arrives and we fall silent while the wait staff serves us. I cannot wait to dig into my sandwich. After they leave, I finish the bite I have taken already and continue, "I was thinking that we could stop by the mall on our way home. Maybe pick up a couple things? I know this," I pluck at my shirt, "was meant for a pale person, not a person with darker skin. I need something more vibrant to set this off. Something I would never have worn before because it would wash me out horribly."

"Yeah it would have, so much. But now you are so changed. I have an idea for the name of your foundation."

I raise an eyebrow and wave for her to go on while I continue stuffing my face.

"You said you wanted it to be magic related, so I started thinking of any name magic related that would come to mind. I must have gone through fifteen or so. World Magic Foundation, Foundation for Magical Beings, all of it. But what I really liked was Foundation for a Magical World. It would still let the magical community guess that we were likely a foundation for the magical community without being terribly overt. What do you think?"

I stopped chewing when she said the name, now I force this chunk of sandwich down, "That name is the one! I love it!"

Natasha opens her mouth to say something else, but frowns as a hand lands on mine. I snatch my hand away and look up to see Charles. "Darling! I have been missing you at the library! So naughty of you to stop working there and not even say a word. I must have gone by there a dozen times looking for you." I glance at Natasha out of the corner of my eye, she is watching the same train way off the tracks as it plows through the countryside of batshit crazy. He just keeps talking as we stand and gather our things to leave, he grabs my arm as we begin to head in, "I heard thru the underground that there is a hit out on you. The killer is here and being as they are already paid, they plan to end your life soon. We should go discuss how best to keep you— AAAGgggghhh!" He releases my arm from his iron grip. His hand is blistered and bright red. I call the wind and a very pointed gust blows him clean across the meadow next to the café. We watch in feigned amazement, to appear the same as the other customers. As they gather to watch him tumble ass over tea kettle across the field, we quietly exit the building.

We make it to the car without actually running and I start the engine; we make it out of the lot in record time while managing not to screech any tires. I tell Natasha, "Call Maggie. We need those bodyguards now." I fiddle with getting my seatbelt on while driving, not my best driver moment, but we had to get far away from that café. Natasha finishes talking to Maggie and hangs up the phone, "She is calling her husband now. She had been putting together a more specialized list for you, but her husband knows them all even better than she does and he will have suitable candidates at the house tomorrow around 1pm. Sound good?"

I laugh, "Sounds like tomorrow is bodyguard interview day."

The next morning we all hurry through our late mornings as none of us are early rising people and haven't been for a long time, though some longer than others. By a quarter to one we are all downstairs in the kitchen, waiting on the arrival of our candidates. We hear the doorbell and Billy walks off to answer the door and show most of them to the sitting room. He takes a very long time before he makes it back to the kitchen with the first one. "There are thirty more where this one came from. I think her husband sent up the wolf signal or something. This," he points to the guy he brought in, "is Gibbs. Steve Gibbs. He says he doesn't appreciate Gibbs jokes, and he smacks a lot harder."

The Gibbs in question glares at Billy as he walks over to lean against a counter. He has more tattoos than I would know what to do with but they are beautiful and don't detract from his looks at all, in fact Natasha seems very taken by his looks. Maybe it is those steel-blue eyes of his, they are mesmerizing.

"Well, let's get this show on the road." I open my notebook and write his name on the first page, "Steve, what jobs have you been working on and what kind of shifter are you?"

At my question he immediately looks toward the floor, a defeated look crosses his face. "Maybe I should go. I don't think I'm qualified to do this. I don't have any training of any kind, and I haven't even worked as a bouncer." He turns to exit the kitchen and I throw a barrier up over the kitchen door, "Hold it right there! I decide, not you. What job you had is not as important as you think. I need to know about you. About your motivations and where your loyalties lie. Your job plays a part in that but is not the sole basis. Please, let us give you a chance." I feel certain I am going to hire him, but I want to know his story before I commit to it. He stopped when I started speaking, and now he turns back around slowly.

He looks suspicious but starts talking, "I work as a field hand. It is the only job I was really qualified for after I got out of the system."

"Why were you in the system? Which system? How old are you?"

He smiles a little at my rapid fire questions, "The foster and juvie systems. My mom died when I was younger, Dad beat her to death. I am twenty."

"You didn't have any relatives to take you in?"

"Dad had family nearby, but they wouldn't take me. Said I would be as much trouble as my Dad. We never found my mom's family. She didn't have any id or anything. It seemed like she ran from them and ended up somewhere worse. So no, I didn't have family that could take me."

"Why did you end up in juvie?"

"Assault."

"What's the rest of the story?"

"I got real sensitive about people hitting girls. It was a trigger for all the rage inside me. It boiled over pretty frequently and I beat the snot out of guys that hit girls. I didn't care why they hit them, but I made sure they weren't going to do it again. Some of the people pressed charges. My fuse was pretty short too. It didn't take much to set me off like the Fourth of July. Once the kids knew that they used it for entertainment. Eventually I met Dario, he works with troubled kids on the side, he helped me get to a better place. When I got out I went to work at a nearby farm, they let me stay as part of my pay. Dario has kept in touch, watched over me all this time."

"How long have you been out?"

"Of juvie? About three years. Foster system? Around two."

"You haven't been fighting since then?"

"I haven't assaulted anyone since then. There have been a few fights."

I hear Devon chuckling softly; I know he approves of Gibbs. I make eye contact with him anyway and he nods with this huge grin on his face.

"Gibbs, you're hired. Natasha, could you show him to a bedroom he can claim as his own?" Natasha smiles widely at Gibbs, and Billy scowls at their retreating backs. Interesting. "Billy, want to bring us another candidate?" He pushes away from the counter and all but stomps out to get the next guy.

I look over at Devon; he shrugs. I suppose Billy will either get over it or say something, eventually.

We spend the rest of the day interviewing people, by the end we have hired four more bodyguards. Brad Rice is a tiger shifter, a little full of himself but a family guy with good values. He is 35 and has been in love with the neighbor girl all his life. Apparently she won't have him because they are different types of shifters. Our other 35-year-old is Owen Stanley. He is a bear shifter, and I was absolutely unsurprised to hear that after he ducked and turned sideways to come in the kitchen. He is really quiet and so gentle, though I don't understand how. He said his family was very poor, and he has been working as a bouncer for a long time to help support them. He was picked on a lot as a child for being so poor. Natasha is adopting him. She linked arms with him as she guided him off to choose his bedroom. I thought Billy would blow a gasket. Last of the guys is John Jennings. He is also the oldest of the group at 55. His eyes are this amazing gray blue and they seem to see everything. He was very reserved and quiet, but unashamed of his background. He has regrets for some choices made that led him to spend time in prison, and that he lost touch with his children while he was in there. He still hasn't found them.

LAST OF ALL IS AJAH STONE. SHE IS A 30-YEAR-OLD BALL of fire. A tiger shifter with no family that she knows of as her parents died shortly after her eighteenth birthday. She is a Jack of all trades and has even done some body work. She worked in various dojos which allowed her to train with them and that still love for her to come by and train with them. I am so thrilled to have her here. A female bodyguard isn't something most people would suspect. She is also going to take on some assistant duties as that will aid in her appearing to be just a girl. Billy didn't get nearly so salty when Natasha walked off in deep conversation with Ajah, I wonder if he would have had he known that Natasha is bisexual?

With all that finished, I call Maggie and thank her and ask her to thank her husband for me. I tell her about the five we hired, she crows with delight when I say Ajah's name, I wait for her to finish so she can explain. She tells me, "Dario lost the bet!" With so much excitement that I ask her what bet he lost. "I said you were going to hire Ajah, that she would be a shoo-in because of her skills and the way people wouldn't see her as a threat. He said no way. Said you all would never hire a black woman with such a weird background. The only reason he sent her is because she happened to overhear him telling someone else and demanded that she get to interview too because she is so damn qualified. I can't wait to tell him that you all aren't racist or sexist assholes! I knew it already, but he doesn't trust people because they are usually so shitty."

I laugh, "Well, I am glad you won the bet. Stick it to him. In the meantime, I should warn you before you see me again… I look a lot different now. My parents were actually my adoptive parents, and they wanted me to look like them so they glamoured me. Grams Griselda removed it yesterday before all the excitement. My hair is a lot darker and my skin is too."

"WHOA. That must have been a hella wild thing to find out. How are you doing with all that?"

"Pretty ok honestly. With that. There are other things that are so out there, but enough of that. Can I like pay you a monthly fee for all the work you do for me? And before you answer that, I have a couple more, much less urgent, posts I need to fill. And I fully intend to keep asking you to do things, but I feel like I should pay you more. You do a lot for me."

"Yes, you can definitely hire me on as a freelancer. I will bill you, and it will be a fair amount. If you don't agree we can negotiate. Sound good?"

I agreed to it and we talked about the positions I need filled now, these for the house. With so many people living here, we need a full-time chef, a couple maids, and somebody to do the damn dusting and answer the door. She laughed at my requests but assured me that she would have a smaller selection of people at my house in three days to be interviewed and that I would have a detailed list of who they were and what their histories/qualifications were landing in my email by the second day. Thanking her, I end the call. Devon steps up behind me and wraps his arms around me from behind. He whispers in my ear, "Everyone is off doing their own thing and we haven't been alone since we woke up this morning. Wanna run upstairs and fool around?"

"Hmm," I wiggle my butt against the firmness in his jeans, "if I run all the way up the stairs I am not going to be able to fool around. It will take me twenty minutes to breathe again."

He steps away and before I can miss the warmth of him, he sweeps me up into his arms saying, "Problem solved." He runs us up the stairs and to our bedroom. He kicks the door shut and sets me on my feet. I tilt as my world spins and he grabs me before I fall. Leaning against his chest is the best feeling ever. "Humans aren't supposed to go that fast. Except in cars. That fast up the stairs is dizzying. Especially with no warning. I almost lost my cookies. Nobody wants that all over them. Regurgitated anything is gross when it lands in your face." I feel his chuckle down in his chest more than I hear it. He asks me, "Should I still be worried about cookie loss or are you good?"

I lean back away from the warmth of his chest with my hands still firmly on his waist. The world is not spinning nearly so much, "I think—" a knock sounds at the door. We both sigh and Devon tells them to come in.

Billy steps in the doorway, "Hey Devon, are— what's going on here? Do you two need some time alone? Should I go?" I open my eyes with the plan to crack a joke when all my cookies rush up and out onto Devon's chest and down to his shoes. "Och, yer no doin' it right if that's her reaction."

"I need tea. Ginger tea. Billy, would you, please?" I croak out with what is left of my throat. There is vomit splattered on the both of us and if it weren't so disgusting it would be hilarious. I feel certain this is going to be a vampire cautionary tale one day.

"Let's get you leaned up against this bed behind you. One step back, I will hold you up. Good job. One more step back, ok. Just lean back a little till your butt touches the bed. Excellent. Get this shirt off you. Here we go. Now the pants, they aren't any better. I'll slide them under your butt and down your legs, you just hold my shoulders while you lift your feet." He is so gentle, even helping me first now that I have covered him in vomit. He carefully places my hands on the bed to either side of me once he has removed my pants. I feel the wind of him going for more clothing. He is back fast, gentle as he tugs my arms into the silken robe. I feel him close the front and tie it shut. I crack one eye just a little to see if it is any better yet, that's a hard no. I close that eye before I can lose my cookies again. I smell the ginger tea as Billy draws near. "Here you go, little one," he takes my hands and puts them around the cup. The heat from the cup is oddly reassuring. "Do you need help drinking it?"

"No, but I wouldn't mind if you kept me company until Devon gets out of the shower. I feel exposed not being able to open my eyes without getting dizzy and feeling like my cookies are going to make another visit."

I feel him lean against the bed, then he asks, "Do you often lose your cookies when you sneak away to the bedroom?"

"What? No! What kind of question is that?"

"Well, most women don't get randomly sick unless they are pregnant."

"Whoa, mister! Hold that train, send it back the other way. He ran me up the stairs. We were coming up to fool around and I told him if I ran it would take me 15-20 minutes to catch my breath so he scooped me up and ran full-on vampire speed. I think I will be fine when all of me finally makes it up the stairs."

Billy is laughing loudly by the time I finish telling him the problem. "He…You…Ahahahahahaha!"

I would roll my eyes, but for the fact that it wouldn't even be seen. "Great. Laugh at my pain. Nobody enjoys tossing their cookies, it does not feel even a little ok."

"I know, I know, I'm sorry. It's just so funny. I think his vampire knowledge is really lacking. That is a rookie mistake."

My ears perk up at this, "Where would one get vampire learning? Is there a manual? You know I plan to become a vampire, where do we learn all the things?"

"Slow down little one, we don't have a book or anything."

"Well, why not? This many vampires on the planet and you can't even create one stinking book?"

"Vampires like to keep their secrets. We don't share things easily."

"Well, that has to change. What if I write the book? Will you teach me the vampire lore and knowledge that you will share for my book?"

Billy is silent for so long I wonder if he has left. Just before I ask, he says, "Yes. For you, I will. On one condition, I insist that it not be a widely published book. You can make only five copies. I don't care about the other vampire knowledge you collect, but if it is in with mine, only the five copies. Are we in agreement?"

"Yes, we are in agreement. Five copies only of the lore and knowledge you provide, excepting that which overlaps that of other vampires. Meaning, if you tell me that the old movie trope about killing the sire kills all those he has sired is true, and then five other vampires tell me the same thing, that doesn't count. Deal?" I stick my hand out in his general direction, I feel him clasp my hand and shake it once before releasing it, "Agreed."

"Does that mean you are going to pester me into the same sort of agreement Fate?" Devon asks as he walks into the room.

"I thought I would ask politely and if you didn't cooperate, I would resort to torture."

Billy starts laughing again, "Fate, please don't ever stop causing him to be speechless. It is priceless in so many ways. Has that tea helped you feel better yet?"

I open one eyelid the smallest bit, ok so far. A little more. A little more. I open that eyelid all the way. Ok, so far. I see Devon and Billy both watching me intently. I open the other lid just as slowly. "I think I might be ok. But I need to try standing up." Devon steps toward me, but I hold up a hand, "No. If I feel woozy, I will fall back on the bed. Let me do this myself." I ease myself up into a standing position so I am fully supporting my own weight. Still feeling okay, I take a step, two, three. "Yes, the tea did the trick and I feel fine. Now, I think perhaps I will go have my own shower. Nothing like vomiting to make one feel unclean."

❧ 5 ❧

"I drive. I don't care how old you are or where you've been. This is my town. I know it best, you've only arrived recently. Get your vampire ass in the passenger seat or you can tell Fate why you didn't get to go." I lock the doors to my car with the button and cover myself in flames in case he has any stupid ideas. Vampires. Stubborn, know-it-all, bossy, and downright annoying to deal with unless they are trying to seduce you. Billy glares at me, arms folded across his chest. I simply tap my foot and study my nails as I wait him out.

"Uggggghhhhh!" He hollers and then walks his butt to the passenger side of my car. Sorry pal, you are not driving my car. I extinguish my flames and get into the driver's seat of my car. Doors shut and my seatbelt fastened, I start the car and we are off. Maggie set up three buildings for us to go have a walk around, see if they were in the range of what we would need for the foundation. I am eager to get this thing started so as I do not spend quite so much time with Billy, he really gets under my skin like no one else. I glance at him out of the corner of my eye, he is through being angry and is now learning the city as we drive through it.

"So the first place is pretty close to Devon and Fate's place, only about 20 minutes down the road." I glance over to see him nodding, "Maggie said it was an insurance building at one point in time, it has been for sale for about three years now. It is overpriced, but she thinks with this market being so slow right now, we could get this for even less than the property itself is worth. Especially with the work we would need to put into it to bring it up to code. She thinks it will be a gut job."

"Hmm, that sounds time consuming."

"It can be. But I think we can get a bunch of experts in the magical community together to do the work and make it all go a lot faster."

"Oh, yes. I forget the rest of the community is often much more willing to work together than vampires are, we tend to be more reticent about showing up to group meetings."

"Ha! I bet. We found that sticking together helps us all to stay hidden much better than if we flounder about on our own. Ah, here we are." I pull up in front of the building, not even bothering with parking space etiquette as the lot is empty. Getting out, I take in the building. Looks like a 3 or 4 story building. Lots of glass, all mirrored during the day. The building itself is gray stone. The doors are all glass. Probably not bulletproof, but that could be changed relatively easily. I look over at Billy who has walked around the car to stand looking at the building with me, "What do you think about this place?" He frowns, "It wouldn't be my first choice."

Curious now, I ask him why. He says, "Because this place is too easy to trap everyone inside and send it all crashing to the ground. All the glass is a defense issue too. Yes, it could be changed to be something much more sturdy, but why go to all that trouble when there are better places out there?"

I nod, "I agree with you on all points. Shall we go on to the next building?"

He smiles at me, "We shall."

TEN MINUTES LATER WE ARE AT THE NEXT BUILDING. THIS one is in the downtown area, and it takes us an additional 20 minutes to find a parking spot. Walking the two blocks back to the building, I tell Billy, "I don't like this place already. We would have to buy two buildings and make one a parking garage."

He chuckles, "A brief walk won't hurt you."

In mock outrage I say, "I have a whole bunch of curves to keep up! They are not going to stick around if I spend all my time hiking to and from my car."

He eyes my form, "You do have a very nice set of curves. T'would be a crying shame to take them away from the world. That's that then. Either two buildings or none a'toll. Here anyway."

We come to a stop in front of the building; it is a good size for here, but not for what we need at all. This one manages to be even less suitable than the one before it. I grab Billy's arm, "Look," I point across the street with my other hand at a woman that is the image of Fate, "that is the woman from the pictures in Charlie's office!"

"We should follow her. See what she is up to. I think that is the one that harassed Fate in the parking lot her last day at the library."

I nod and checking traffic first; we hurry across the street and trail behind her. Not long after we start following her, she steps into a restaurant. I look at Billy, "You should buy me lunch."

He raises an eyebrow at me, "If I buy it's a date and you would have to act like you enjoy my company. Think you can manage that?"

Slipping my arm through his, I smile up at him as I lean in close to whisper in his ear, "Think you can manage charming?" The shiver that runs through his body is totally gratifying. He clears his throat, "I think I might be able to manage that." We walk in and arrange to be seated behind the guest of the lady that looks like Fate. One tiny spell on my part and we can hear their conversation while we appear to be leaning in close to talk to each other. Billy is facing toward them, so he is keeping an eye on them in case they start paying attention to us or looking like they are trying not to notice us. The waitress takes our order and I am so grateful that I remembered to set the spell so that we are the only ones able to hear what is being said. We order burgers and fries; simple and quick to make. The two at the table behind me seem to be discussing how best to kill Fate. One of them knows the original layout of the house we are living in very well. They don't seem to be aware that Billy and I are living there, nor do they appear to know about the shifters. The two finish their meal and fight about the check. The fake Fate is really broke right now, and the other lady is not terribly caring. They finally agree on the other lady paying just as we finish our meal. The waitress brings our check over as she collects their card, Billy throws cash on the table and we wander outside slowly after I dissipate the spell. We stroll out of view of the windows. I tell Billy, "We should probably embrace or something if we are going to loiter here, just so we don't look suspicious." He smiles, white teeth brilliant against his black skin, "If you want to kiss me all you have to do is say so. I would never pass up a chance to kiss a beautiful woman like you Natasha." His arms circle me and I have never felt so safe and hot as I do right this minute. His body pressed against mine is setting fires in places that should be unaffected by a guy I don't even like. I look up at him in surprise. His pupils are dilated, and he pulls me closer, I watch his lips as they drift closer to my own. I know I should push him away, but my arms creep around him and pull him closer. Our lips touch and a thousand little explosions happen all over my body. I can't stop kissing this man. We finally break away from each other for lack of oxygen and he looks just as surprised as I am. "I, erm, ahem," I clear my throat as a pause to gather my thoughts, "I think we missed her."

He looks around, "Missed who? OH! Shit. We should call Fate and Devon. I'll call him and you got her, right?" I nod as I dig out my phone. Holy Hera, I don't need this in my life right now.

Fate answers after the third ring and I tell her about seeing the fake Fate and what we overheard, as well as the fact that we lost her. She asks how and I tell her, "Let's talk about that later, ok?"

"Sure, will you be home soon?"

"We have one more building to look at and then we will be along home." We say our goodbyes after that and hanging up the phone I look over at Billy, already done with his call and waiting on me, "We have one more building to look at, think you can keep your hands off me for that?" I grin when his jaw drops and I laugh as I start the hike toward the car. He is quickly beside me, "I can keep my hands to myself. How about you? Pretty sure I have scorch marks on my shirt…" I try to look at his shirt without being too obvious, definitely scorch marks all over it. I can only imagine what my clothing must look like. I ask him, "Being as I am full of fire and you are a vampire, I don't understand why you aren't running far away from me now that I have left scorch marks all over your shirt."

He laughs, "The fire never touched me. Just my clothing." Jumping in front of me, he stops and I nearly plow into him. Steadying me, he leans down to whisper in my ear, "Everyone dies eventually. If today is my day, what a way to go." My eyes drift closed and my head tilts to give him better access to all the sensitive areas on my neck. He kisses the spot where my neck and shoulder meet, this time I am the one shivering as he draws back. "You said we have another house to look at today. I hope you don't date many vampires." He turns and starts toward the car once again. I take a few quick steps to catch up to him, "What do you mean you hope I don't date many vampires?"

He grins at me again, "Because you would be easy prey with a neck like that. One little whisper near your ear and suddenly you have your head tilted off to one side, that gorgeous caramel neck bared, begging for teeth and lips."

I flush. He's right. Good grief. No wonder I see so many of them, they probably love the hell out of that reaction. "Um, I would like to say no, never, but I'm not a liar. I hang with them on a regular basis. Guessing that is part of why they love me." I shrug, as a way to dismiss it. Most guys run away from a woman as free with her sexuality as I am, but I figure that just helps me weed out the losers. The vampires I have met had no issues, most of them wanted to turn me and keep me as a long-term partner, but I haven't been into that. Now that Fate is going to be turned, well, maybe I will take someone up on that offer. I don't care if I change men like my underwear, a good girl-friend is hard to come by. I have never liked the idea of chancing it that I would eventually find a female vampire that I could be as close with as I am with Fate and Memré. I like to think I am close to Pru, but I had no idea she had so little ethics about her abilities, I wonder what she actu-ally thinks of me?

We make it to the car and head off to the last place. Billy keeps looking over at me. It's making me antsy, "Would you just spill already? What's on your mind Billy?"

"After I said that about vampires, you answered and got really quiet. Deep in thought and the thoughts looked unhappy. If my comment caused that, I apologize."

"Your comment didn't cause it so much as my own thoughts and dealing I have had with others in the past. I appreciate that you did not intend it in a hurtful way. You're good, Billy. All these issues are my own. Here is the place. Maggie said this was the one she thought we would love. It has tons of space, multiple buildings, covered walkways, and some of the buildings are already set up for children. This used to be a government building, but they moved on into two larger sets of buildings. The child friendly buildings held daycares for the children of mothers still in high school so that they could continue their education, lack of childcare being a lot of the reason why teen mothers drop out of high school." We walk the warren of covered walkways through the buildings, there are twenty separate buildings in various sizes. The parking lot circles the place, with a few islands for trees. As we head back to the car Billy asks me, "What do you think about this place?"

"I think it is perfect. Pretty easy to throw a boundary around if we need to, and so much space. It is in town without being crowded by everything, she could buy the lots on three sides to ensure it stays that way. It looks like any work needed will be minimal and mostly cosmetic. In short, it's perfect."

"I agree. Think Fate will take our suggestion?"

"I know she will. Fate isn't experienced with all this, but she wouldn't have wasted everyone's time sending us out to look at it if she didn't feel like we could make the choice for her."

❦ 6 ❧

"**D**evon, are you aware that I can in fact hang you from the rafters without ever touching you?" He freezes mid-tirade, "Yes, but I am going to be very mad if you do."

going to be very mad if you do."

I step out of the reach of his arms; I know he is thinking he will cuddle me into his way of thinking, but that ship was never in port. I hold up a hand to stop him advancing, "What do you think it will take for me to hang you up in the rafters? I sure as hell don't do it for fun. Get it through your thick skull — Hi Natasha, Billy!"

Devon spins around to greet the two standing in the doorway to the sitting room. Both raise their eyebrows at him and I invite them to come sit so we can all discuss things.

Devon sits on the love seat with me and scooches as close as he can get. He hates it when I am mad at him. I am not actually mad, I simply want him to realize that I am a whole person and considering as I have all my memories and experiences from all of my lives, including the ones before him, I am mentally much older than he is and my decision making is perfectly sound.

We go over what they heard Fake-me talking about again, both Natasha and Billy look wildly uncomfortable talking about the how and why they lost her. I let it go after giving Natasha a look; she nodded. It was so small that had I not been watching, I couldn't have sworn she nodded.

"Fate, love, this is all too much. You should put the business on hold. Wait till things calm down before you do all the work it will take to push this through."

"Bite me." Everyone turned to stare at me, Devon asked, "What did you say?"

"I said, BITE ME. I mean that metaphorically and literally. If you think I am pausing my life because there are assholes everywhere, you can metaphorically bite me. If you would like to help by turning me now, that would be great and you could literally bite me. Are we cleared up now? Or shall I further elucidate on the subject for you?"

Devon stands, turns toward me and back toward the door. He does this a few times before he leaves the room entirely.

I do not understand what is going on with him. I look over to Billy for answers, "Why won't he go ahead and turn me already? Or let someone else do it for crying out loud?"

Billy shrugs, "You got me. If it was my choice, you would have been turned less than five minutes after you decided you wanted it done. I mean, it really is so much safer for you. You get way stronger, faster, your senses go through the roof unless you lost them before you were turned. And in your case, you would also still be a witch. I mean, you wouldn't need backup for most things. You would be your own backup. I bet it would be amazing to watch you take out some assholes. Maybe we should try talking to him about it separately? See if he can talk to one of us if it is one on one?"

I tap my fingers on the arm of the loveseat, "I suppose. It may be the best way. I really need his support on this and I think it would make most things so much easier if I were a vamp. Let's all talk to him, maybe he will come clean with whatever is bothering him about this whole mess. In the meantime, tomorrow is maid interview day. Who wants in on that?"

Natasha is first to speak, "I do. I don't want some pushy person running around here rearranging my panty drawer because they don't like the way I do it. I want them to be well aware that we are allowing them into our personal spaces to do as we ask, not impose their will upon us. I arrange my things the way I like, I don't want it constantly changed to suit someone else's taste."

"I think I would like to be there as well, just to sniff out anything strange." Billy tells me as he stretches, "We don't need another like the last maid he had and I heard all about her when she was sent out of here. I think I am off to get a nap. Wake me if you need anything."

He smiles at Natasha and she blushes a bright red.

"Excellent, now tell me what is going on with that." I say, pointing toward the doorway recently vacated by Billy.

"I don't want to talk about it just yet, I don't really know myself what is going on. How about I tell you when I know something?"

I sigh with a dramatic flair, "I suppose that will have to do." And then fall back on the couch as though passed out. Natasha laughs at me and we both leave the room, heading for our own spaces.

$\approx$ 7 $\approx$

The next day dawns entirely too early. It seems like I just fell asleep and already it is nearly 11. Devon is stroking my face gently as he says my name to wake me. I smile at him, happy to wake up to his face. "Wake up sweetheart, we have interviews today." I nod and stretch, "Ok, I'm up. Are you making coffee this morning?"

"It is made, waiting for you downstairs."

I lean over and give him a kiss, "You are a king among vampires, love, and I am the luckiest woman on the planet. I'll be down in a minute. The bathroom is singing me the siren song of morning tinkles." He laughs as he wanders off downstairs and I tend to emptying my very full bladder. While I wait for the falls to run dry, my brain starts turning.

I have enjoyed these few short weeks more than any other time in my entire life; I hope this never ends. I am terrified that it actually might end, between Charles and this killer and whatever the fake Fate has in store for me. I don't want to start over again. I love this body; it isn't perfect by any means and right now some of it is pretty new to me, but I love this body. I want to keep it. I need to talk to Devon about turning me. There is no good reason for him not to turn me unless he is keeping something from me? I mean, I guess that is possible. The falls finally run dry and I take care of business, wash my hands, and head downstairs. Coffee is a necessity for all the interviews we have planned today. At least we will finally have some help around the house. Every one of us is out running around or working from here most of every day. I step into the kitchen and the aroma of coffee wraps around me like a hug from a dear relative. Devon has made a cup for me and set it on the counter next to where he leans drinking his own coffee. What a gorgeous site to behold. I sidle up next to him, scooping up my cup as I do. I slowly raise the cup and smell the coffee before taking that first hot sip. Divine.

I manage to get the coffee in me, get showered and get dressed in time to make it down the stairs as the first interview for maid is being shown into the kitchen. She is young, blond, sickly Victorian child pale, and really quite lovely. She has an ethereal quality about her. I am thinking she will be great. She sees me and I smile at her, "Welcome! My name is Fate, you are?" I hold my hand out toward her as I walk closer to her and Billy, she looks me up and down before asking Billy in an icy tone, "Is all the help so informal? I am used to working for a more formal clientele." My jaw drops. Did she really just decide I was a maid? I look down at my clothing, I am wearing a nice dark skirt, an emerald green silk blouse, and a pair of ballet flats. I even did my damn hair and makeup.

I look back up at her, "What exactly makes you think I am the help?"

The sickly Victorian looks between Billy and I, suddenly seeming very uncomfortable. Billy has crossed his arms and taken a step back, quite content to let this child sink or swim all on her own. Based on his reaction, I have an idea of her motives, but I want to see what she actually says.

"Well, you seem very casual in your dress… And overly friendly… It seemed like you were an employee."

I raise an eyebrow at her, "I am dressed well for most offices. Overly friendly? What? Try again honey and I advise you to tell the truth."

The Victorian child grits her teeth, "Fine. I didn't expect a brown woman to be in charge in this house, in this neigh-borhood. It isn't the norm and also, brown families aren't usually well off enough to be able to pay a housekeeper, much less a head housekeeper over staff."

Billy has stepped back once again, as though he feels I might decide to injure the child and he wishes to be well out of the danger zone. I take a moment to breathe and cross my arms. Exhaling, I ask the child, "Do you know what is wrong with everything you just said?"

She shrugs, "It was incorrect?"

My eyes roll of their own accord, "I am very sorry, you are not right for the position. Your racism is showing and you haven't been here five minutes. Billy, please show the child back out, her interview is complete."

The sickly Victorian child begins to splutter about the Better Business Bureau and filing complaints. "You have displayed racist behavior before we could even interview you and your behavior is threatening. I will have no problems defending my decision, however you may have problems getting hired when word of your behavior gets out. Have a nice day, child."

Natasha and Ajah have come out now to see what the commotion is, and they tell Billy that they will escort her out. He looks surprised but acquiesces. The two women each take one of the child's arms and guide her toward the front door. Billy strolls over and offers an arm, I take it and we walk toward the kitchen together.

"She looked like trouble when I opened the door, but I figured we had to at least give her a chance to be interviewed."

I nod, "Your instincts were completely on point. She is nothing but trouble. I am really glad that Natasha and Ajah walked her out, who knows what she would have tried to accuse you of doing in order to get revenge on us. Which, I am sorry to say, did not at first occur to me."

He laughs as we walk into the kitchen, "Its all good, I have been in worse situations. Just ask Devon here about how mad folks get when hanging doesn't work and they see you walking around a couple weeks later."

"Oh my, that happened?" My eyes may fall out and roll across the floor, they are so bugged right now. The two men nod and Billy says, "Yes. I know you aren't used to being darker, and you were closer to the color of the woman that left until very recently, but this kind of thing happens all the time. You may wish for that glamour back before all is said and done."

I shake my head, blinking fast. "No." I reach Devon's side and he puts an arm around me, "I don't even know if I can forgive them for glamouring me like that. I mean, I am not even that dark. Why would they glamour me to look so much different after they sought me out?"

Devon gives me a squeeze, "It could be anything. But they are dead, and we are not likely to find out anytime soon. It sounds like Natasha and Ajah are coming back with the next candidate, let's get this done."

We spend the next few hours interviewing candidates. As it turns out the first girl was named Emily and she was a fairy. The next five were witches, and two of them were only here to get gossip in person. They didn't even want the job. Two wolves and then an owl shifter named Marina Munoz. Marina was by far the most qualified and best applicant. The last two wolves seemed competent but had no experience, after talking with Marina we decided to give her the head housekeeping position and hire the two inexperienced wolves as well. Marina wanted the help, and she said she would rather train those without experience to do it right than re-train those that were taught to do it wrong. We thought that was a splendid plan and asked her what she thought about the wolves, Sheri and Nicki. She said they got along great while waiting for their interviews and they would be perfect. Natasha called them right then and asked them to come back if they wanted jobs. Both were back at the house within ten minutes.

Devon and I take the three on a tour of the house, showing them where everyone sleeps and discussing the things we want done and what we want left alone. We introduce them to Ajah and Steve, telling them that John, Owen and Brad are off duty at the moment. My office is not part of their duties. We make sure they know that we tend toward later hours and that we prefer most things to operate around that later schedule. Devon tells them we have plans to bring in a chef and Marina cuts him off, "You don't need to, unless you prefer all the duties be separate. I am an excellent cook and for a small raise I would be happy to oversee meals too."

Devon looks at me, and I shake my head yes quite vigorously. "That is perfect. I will add the chef pay to yours, and I will boost your pay as well," he waves a hand in the direction of Sheri and Nicki, "as I feel certain that you will be part of the kitchen staff too."

We finish up touring the house, showing them the rooms they are welcome to use if they choose to stay here. We make it very clear that staying is absolutely not a job requirement, only a perk if they choose and as they choose. The trio leave for the night with a promise to return tomorrow by 11. They all seem thrilled with being hired and I hope they will be happy working with us.

Devon and I head back to the kitchen after they leave. We put together a veggie, cheese and meat plate for our lunch. We set up an entire tray with the plate and sweet tea, taking it out the back to a small patio area shaded by a wisteria-covered pergola. It has been a busy week and we have barely had time to kiss each other passing in the hallway, much less talk to each other.

Sitting out in the sweetly scented breeze sharing a meal and conversation is just what we needed. I tell him about our Pru problems, and he is less than surprised. I am surprised by his lack of surprise and I ask him about it.

Devon shrugs as he picks apart a piece of turkey, "Well, when I met her that day she was careful to be nice in front of all of you, but she also spent a lot of time trying to get into my head. Even when you were working through all the revelations about Charlie, she was working to crack my mental walls. I have been thinking ever since then, how much did she know about Charlie that you didn't know? What other secrets is she privy to that could hurt you. I didn't want to say anything until you knew she was like that and I was really hoping you would see it soon. But as a precaution I have had Billy and your bodyguards watching her too. I also trained the bodyguards in how to keep her out, though they didn't need it. She apparently hasn't even tried with them."

My jaw is hanging by the time he finishes speaking. The things I don't know have just been piling up by the wayside. Wow. I close my mouth and shake my head to clear it. My sister is a kind of horrible that I thought was special to me, but it turns out that she has been doing this to everyone that she thinks is equal to her. "I… I am so sorry Devon. All these years it never occurred to me that she would do this to other people, I… Damn. Well, Grams gave us a way to take care of that too. She passed a spell to us that will stop any mind reader from accessing our minds and another to bind Pru if she can't… or won't change."

Devon's eyes widen, "Wow. The few witches I have known don't break that kind of firepower out for much of anything. Are you sure you want to do that?"

I shake my head no, "Of course I don't want to do that to her. Even with all the things she has done, she is still my sister. I love her. I can't imagine what it would be like to have my powers locked away from me. But I have a responsibility to not allow her to continue to invade people's minds. The lack of ethics on her part is horrifying." I feel my eyes burn and I start fast blinking, I hate crying. Swallowing down my discomfort, I continue, "If there is any way to avoid this I will. But I have to protect the innocent. All the people she is mentally raping. It can't go on. Tonight we will cast the spell to block all mind readers from accessing our minds on everyone in the house. I will call Pru and talk with her, see if she is willing to change."

"What if she isn't willing? How would we know?"

"Ah, well, Grams held the answer for that too. She said that we would still feel that she was trying to get in our minds, it just wouldn't hurt when she tried to break in. So we will know when she comes around and tries to break into my mind." The idea that I would have no choice but to bind my sister broke my heart in two. Fast blinking would not stop these fat tears rolling down my face. Devon takes my hand in his, giving it a little squeeze. I appreciate the comfort and the space to feel these feelings. I don't want to mess up my shirt, so I do grab a napkin to keep the tears from falling off my face.

Once the tears have dried up Devon and I move on to happier topics, just to enjoy the rest of our lunch without letting the world and our problems intrude. The food gone, we collect our mess and take it all back into the kitchen. Natasha, Billy, Ajah and Steve are all in there as we come in. Natasha looks at my face and shoots me a questioning look, I wave it away so she knows it is just all the stuff. She nods, "Ready to get to work?" I kiss Devon and say, "Let's go."

I stop just outside the kitchen, "Oh hey, Ajah, Steve;" the two look over from their own lunches, "I plan to go clothing shopping later, I probably should take you two with me." Devon nods hard enough I wonder if his head will fly off and bounce across the floor. I smile at him, it is cute that he worries. Be cuter if he would turn me into a vampire already. The two nod, saying they will be ready when I am. I thank them and continue up to my office.

Natasha is waiting outside the barrier for me when I enter, we clasp hands and enter the warded area together. The book waits on the lectern, and the other one sits in silent reproach on the table next to it. Natasha opens her laptop and I run my hands over the book. It would upset most librarians. My bare hands on the book however, in this case, damage from the oils in my hands is not a concern. All witches spell their grimoires to protect them from such things as incidental dirts, or oils, or potion spills. Explosions. That kind of thing. Never against fire though, that practice is a tradition from a time that held dangerous consequences if your house burnt down and a book inside did not. That could get the owner of the book burnt in the town square.

I open the book slowly, my time studying these books and getting to appreciate them is incredibly special to me. It feels almost sacred. I take a deep breath, grimoire always smell of the things that were used around them most. This one smells of sweet incense and pungent charcoal. A family of air witches. That explains why they would have the sort of spell inside that Grams wanted us to have. Air witches are most closely connected with the mind and things of the mind. Being mentally raped by a mind reader would be doubly awful for them. I skim the spells and other entries, paging through the book quicker than I like because we do need to get this spell found so we can cast it later, after we find me some clothing. Natasha has great taste, but I want my own clothing.

About halfway in I find the first spell, "Here it is!" I tip the book up and hold it in place while Natasha takes a quick picture. She sends it to print and looks over the image on her phone saying, "It looks like we have everything we need to do this." Setting the book back down, I tell her, "That was what I saw as well. We have all the supplies to get this done as soon as we come back from shopping."

Natasha purses her lips, "We could do that. But if we run into Pru while we are out… Well, that is likely to be very awkward. I think we should cast it before we go. At least on us, Ajah, and Steve. Since we will be out in public where Pru could happen to be out."

I nod my head, looking back at the spell. It looks like it will take maybe 2 minutes for this. "Ok. Everyone in the house now gets the spell and we will put it on the rest when we see them."

I SEND OUT A MESSAGE FOR EVERYONE IN THE HOUSE TO meet us in the parlor, Natasha grabs the printout and the two bundles of herbs we need for the spell. Downstairs everyone is in the parlor waiting for us. Natasha and I grabbed our purses on the way downstairs, so we can leave as soon as we finish up here. She lights the bundles; three plants total. She walks around the outside of the group while I make a circuit of the inside. As we walk, we speak the words of the spell:

Smoke of Floramon
Round the mind
Seed of Amaranth
Create the shell
Sweet Wood of Fire
Seal the spell

THE ROOM SEEMS TO FILL WITH A GLOWING MIST, AND then like a flash it is gone. Natasha and I put out our bundles and I walk over to Devon who is just standing up. "Love, we are going to go do some shopping. Get some clothes that work better with my coloring than the stuff I wore when I was pale." Ajah and Steve follow Natasha out to the car while I kiss Devon goodbye. He places his hands on either side of my face, "Please be careful, extra careful. For me?"

I smile at him, "I will. Now I have to go so I can get back and show you how much I missed you." I hurry out the door and hop in the backseat of the Suburban.

❧

FIFTEEN MINUTES LATER, WE PULL UP TO THE SOUTH POINT mall. I spot the Apple store as we are walking in and I can't resist. I walk in and start talking to them about my first Mac. The sales people are outstanding and it thrills Natasha when I get her a MacBook for work. We get the order in and arrange for shipping, because they are making these to our specifications. Leaving the Apple store Natasha says, "No more stalling, straight to Nordstrom's with you." She guides me through the mall, unerring in her direction. I get the feeling she may have been here once or twice. I have never been inside a Nordstrom store, I was never overly concerned with looking nice. I suppose Natasha is taking advantage of the fact that I have no choice but to change out of my wardrobe. Once in the store she lets go and I follow her as she picks up things she says I am trying on.

I am in so much trouble.

Ajah and Steve are snickering behind me, I turn and glare at them, "We could get uniforms."

They stop visibly laughing, but their eyes still dance with merriment. Nothing for it, I suppose. I follow Natasha and her armload of clothes off to the dressing room.

The dressing rooms here are huge. Natasha walks in with me, Steve and Ajah stand guard outside the dressing room area. I strip and start with trying on the dresses she chose. I get the first one on and turn to look in the mirror when she says, "Nope. Not that one. Take it off, don't even look at it."

"Sure thing Mom…"

Natasha laughs and then in a more serious tone she asks me, "How are you doing with all this? Are you okay?"

I poke my head out of the neckline of the next dress, "Yeah, I'm fine mostly. I am loving the deep olive color of my skin, the way my hair is actually dark and way thicker than I ever thought possible. My bod is rockin'. I am having problems with the idea that my parents were so horrid. They covered up who I am, prevented me from being me, and it kind of looks like it was because I wasn't white enough for them. Then all the stuff with Pru… It's just a lot to try to process it all. I went from thinking I had these great parents that loved me and unfortunately died early to everything is up in the air. My biggest question is why, and I don't know if I will ever get an answer."

Natasha nods, "That dress is great, goes with the keeper pile. I can understand that it would turn me upside down too. Do you think Pru has any answers she might be willing to share? I mean, maybe she knows things that she lifted from their minds. The problem, wait. Take that one off. If it is that much of a pain to get into you don't need it. Here, try this one, then you can move on to the other stuff. As I was saying, the problem with training a mind reader to monitor the minds of everyone around her is that she is likely to monitor yours too. She may know a lot of things that your parents didn't really want you or anyone else to know about."

"I hadn't even thought about that. Maybe Pru knows things. Wait, my mom had a diary all her life. I wonder what happened to that when she died? I bet Pru has it. I think I would rather get what I can from that than to benefit from her mind raping my parents. That just doesn't sit right with me. No matter the reason for it."

Natasha nods and hands me an outfit, "I can understand that. I lost sight of that in light of the idea that you could have some answers. But they are dead and if this is what they taught her to do then maybe it isn't such a terrible thing if Pru decides to share it with you? Maybe you don't seek it out, but if Pru tells you some of it then maybe you just let her?"

I look up from buttoning the pants, "Well, maybe? I think it may be a moot point though, I feel pretty certain that she is going to be really mad when I tell her that she has to change her mind raping ways or pay the price."

I like this outfit, and I hand it over to the keep pile. I try on two more outfits, and I made it through the pile. Phew! Natasha is a whirlwind when she shops, but she is amazing at finding the right clothes. Wow. We have been silent since my last statement, Pru is weighing heavily on our minds. We get all the clothes back on hangers and head out to the attendant. She takes the ones that are a pass and we continue on to the checkout.

After charging an exorbitant amount of money to my card, we exit Nordstroms, one enormous bag in hand. Steve and Ajah both offered to carry it for me, but I told them I should carry it in case we run into a murderer. More difficult for them to protect me if they are carrying the bags.

Back in the Suburban, Natasha and I are a little exhausted. Maybe we should leave the heavy topics for days when we aren't shopping.

❈ 8 ❈

Today is the day. I might just get some answers about Charlie and what happened with our marriage. Why did he want to have me killed? Who were all those women in the pictures? Are they all still alive? I mean, I know at least one of them is alive and mad about me inheriting all the things she thought would be hers. Natasha is going with me for moral support and Ajah is coming for bodyguard duties, since we are only going to Ben's office I feel like there is no need for two bodyguards. I really love my bodyguards, but I hate that I need them.

❧

Walking into Ben's office, his receptionist greets me, "Fate! How wonderful to see you! He is expecting you, go ahead in."

"Thanks Beth!" I lead the way, Natasha and Ajah follow me in. I told Ajah it was up to her whether or not she came in, but she wouldn't be able to talk about any of this with anyone but us. She told me she didn't have any friends to speak of and that wouldn't be a problem. I hugged her, because that is hard for anyone. Ben walks around his desk and hugs each of us in turn as we come in. Sitting back down at his desk, he sighs, "I know you need to watch these videos. Since I know a little more about Charlie now, I have set up a private room for you to view them in. Your friends are welcome if you want them. There is space. I wanted you to have privacy for this. Have you read those letters yet?"

"Crap. No. I forgot about them with everything else going on. I will read them soon. I need to get to these videos though, before I lose my nerve." Natasha rubs small circles on my back, not sure if the comfort is for me or her.

Ben nods and getting up he leads the way out of his office and down the hall. At the last door on the left he stops and opens the door, stepping in and holding it open while he waits for us to file in. There is a small memory type box on the table, four chairs, a tv on the wall, and a dvd/bluray player under that on a small floating shelf.

"The disks are in the box, make yourself at home here. If you need tissues Beth has a box. Stay as long as you like, no one will disturb you."

The three of us wait for the door to close before walking over to sit down. I take the middle chair, with Natasha and Ajah sitting to the left and right of me, respectively. Ajah said she wanted to be closer to the door in case of issues. I reach out and pull the box to me. Taking a deep breath, I pull the lid up and off, setting it to the side. There are four disks in the box. The one on top is labeled Fate in Charlie's handwriting.

I lift it out and Natasha takes it from me; she walks over to the player and pops the disk in, turning on the television and bringing back the remote control. I look back in the box, the next disk is labeled Amalia. Who the hell is Amalia? I lift the remaining disks out of the box, the other two are labeled 'Where to Find' and 'If Fate Dies After Me'. These things are not reassuring in any way.

I lay the three disks on the table in front of me; I hear Natasha gasp as she sees the labels.

"Go ahead and press play on this one. I feel like these will be very enlightening."

She eyes me briefly but presses play.

Charlie's face appears on the screen and I have an irrational urge to slap him silly. He appears to be checking to make sure things are working as they should before he begins. Settling into his chair, he takes a breath and begins to speak, "Hello Fate. If you are watching this, then somehow I managed to die before you. That was not what

I intended at all, as you probably know by now, considering as you have likely gone through my office, though I had forbidden you to enter the room while I was alive, well, I don't suppose that really holds any weight once I am dead. I imagine you have a lot of questions and I feel like if you have outlived me, I probably owe you at least some of those answers.

So here goes. First, the reason why I didn't want you using your magic at home was a deal I made with your parents. They were actually terrified that you would grow to be a menace and do something terrible. I told them there was no worry about that—"

"Pause it! Pause it! I need a minute!" My face is leaking like a sieve at this point and my hand is on my heart that is breaking in my chest. Natasha scrambles to pause the disk with fingers that don't seem to be working right this minute, but she gets the video paused. "Why? Why would my parents think that? What did I do that made them think so badly of me?"

Natasha reaches over to hug me, telling Ajah, "Please get those tissues, we gonna need a box." I hear her leave as I rest my forehead on Natasha's shoulder, in an attempt to not mess up her shirt. She pats my back and murmurs soothing things while I cry over the loss of the fantasy of my parents. "I know there were definite signs that something was off with my parents, but I was sure that I was making too much out of what I was seeing. I realize that I just didn't want to see that they didn't like me, much less love me. I was this burden they had to bear and I don't know what to do with this feeling!" Ajah has come in and she thrusts a wad of tissues under my face, I take them from her and try to clean my face a little. Mostly the snot, the tears aren't ready to stop. Natasha keeps rubbing my back, I can see that Ajah has knelt down next to me, ready with more tissues should I need them. She has a wastebasket between her knees too, which is great. I don't want to put my snot rags in anyone's hands. The tears dry eventually. "It's funny, all the stuff I am sure to learn about him, I don't care. I know he wanted me dead. I know he hired someone who is out there now and still trying to get the job done. None of that matters. My parents feeling like I was a threat to the world, that completely breaks me."

Natasha and Ajah both tell me that after all I have been through, that was probably the last straw. Natasha goes on, "Nobody should have horrible parents. But, in this case, I would like to point out that at least they were adoptive parents. Obviously your parents were trying to save you from something by sending you to the nun in Armenia. Your parents cared enough about you to send you away, and that is a big thing. That is enormous love. So whatever was wrong with these idiots, somewhere out there you have someone that loves you enough to send you to safety. Let's cling to that for a minute while you process the shithole behavior?"

I laugh, "Yeah, you're right. Thank you both," I say as I sit back, drop my tissues into the basket and take the ones Ajah has ready for me, "I really appreciate you being here, I couldn't do this without the two of you." I take a deep breath, "Ok, let's get this show on the road. Keep those tissues handy, Ajah, I may need them again." Natasha hits play and Charlie animates again.

"As you were so easy to control. So I laid down the law and no magic in the house. I moved you away from your magic friends," Natasha flips the on-screen Charlie her middle finger, "so you would be less tempted even. You were so closed off from everything that you never even noticed what I was doing. I never loved you, you were a trophy. Once your parents passed away, I hired good old Maude to kill you. She has your entire schedule and knows all your habits. You are sooo predictable. Of course, she may have already gotten you, and if it is Amalia watching, love you honey. If not, well, Fate, have an enjoyable life. While it lasts.

If you are lucky, you will find all the money I hid away. There is a chunk that came from your parents."

"PAUSE!"

Natasha had her finger on the button this time. She hit the button before I finished the word.

"He got a chunk of money from my parents? What the hell? That means Pru knew he got that, and she never said anything! Wow, even my sister is not someone I can trust! I mean, I know she is a dirty mind-raper, but for some reason I didn't connect that with her not having my best interests at heart. Like I thought maybe she was a little brainwashed by our parents and would be ok. Oh, man. I am not going to have a choice, am I Natasha?"

She nods, "Not likely. I am so sorry."

"Hit play. Maybe he will tell me where it is now."

"They gave their attorney very specific instructions about how to handle things and they left Pru and myself both sizable sums of money, and Pru got the house too, being their only actual daughter. Did you know that Fate? Did you know you weren't even their daughter, just some brat they adopted out of Armenia because you had air magic like some of their family did? Well, that is what happened. That is why when you suggested the DNA testing a few years back I vetoed it. Your sister has already done hers and that would have shown the two of you as not being related. It would have been inconvenient for you to know that right then.

So, whoever is watching this, that chunk of money is in a large deposit box at the Latino Credit Union. They didn't like me, and it pleased me to tweak their noses by using my money to get what I wanted. It is the biggest box they had, and the key is hidden in your box Fate. Yes, the one you had hidden from me. Your sister told me all about it one day while you were gone and we were laughing about you. We both found it hilarious to hide the key in the one place you would never look, your own magic box.

Die well, Fate."

The video ends, leaving all three of us sitting there stunned. There is just so much to process. I snatch my phone out of my purse and send out a group text to all the bodyguards, Marina and her two helpers, Devon, Billy, and Memré.

Pru is not who she seems to be, do not allow her in the house and do not meet with her anywhere. She is not to be trusted.

I immediately get texts back outside of the group from Devon, Billy, and Memré.

They all sent some version of what is going on and I sent back to each of them messages saying that I would explain fully later. To Memré I also asked if she would come over for dinner so I could do the explaining to everyone at the same time.

Everyone okayed my plans for later explanations and dinner. One more text to let Marina know there would be an extra mouth for dinner. Natasha and Ajah read over my shoulder as these texts flew back and forth. I held the phone out a bit so that they could see more easily.

"Ok. Let's get the one labeled Amalia in there. See what he had to say to her. Maybe he has even more hidden away. Not that I am going to share anything with her, but I don't want to leave these things lying around unattended."

Ajah grabs the disk and switches them out, Natasha waits for her to be seated before she hits play on this one.

Charlie appears on the screen once again, when he gets settled his face transforms, "Amalia my love, I am so sorry you are watching this. Please know I never wanted to leave you. You know I hired Maude to take care of Fate, I have made the payment. She knows you are her contact if I should disappear. If Fate has not already watched these videos, then I have things squirreled away for you. I did this just in case. There are deeds to three properties, including the one you live in, along with five hundred thousand sitting in a lockbox at the North Carolina Museum of Natural Sciences. The code is 08-64-97. The locker is number 78. You will need to show Fate's ID to get in to the locker area. Break into my office, the ID cards are in the same place, tucked into the drawer box, just pull the drawer out and they will fall out. You will need a lot of the papers in that drawer as well. Maybe just take the whole drawer along with the ID's?

I want you to be happy love; I hope it is you watching these videos and that you are living your best life. My biggest regret is that I did not out live Fate and get to have the pleasure of being married to you. As you know, I could never trust her sister. She knew too much. If I had divorced Fate, she might have decided to side with Fate to take my money. Wait till she finds out I paid Maude to kill her too, but only after Fate dies. I love you so much, Amalia; I hope you never have reason to see this video. Oh, there is also information in the locker about where to find the other stashes I squirreled away for you love. I will end this now and hope that you never have to see it. I love you, Amalia.

Fate, if you are watching this, go die already."

The video ends and we are all left staring at the screen in shock. He is just so blatantly awful. The whole reason he wanted me to die was because of the money? Some of which came from my parents, anyway? Holy shit. This is so beyond anything I would have ever expected. Why did he marry me even? I mean, he pursued me... So weird. I may never fully know. Unless Pru comes clean, but I can't really trust anything she says either.

Ajah grabs the disk labeled 'Where to Find' and swaps it with the one in the player. Natasha immediately hits play and we all lean forward to watch. This is all so wild. Charlie appears once again, "Well, hopefully it is Amalia watching this. Fate, if you are watching, please pass this on to her. I know you don't owe her anything and you are probably really mad, but none of this is her fault.

Amalia love, get your phone out. I want you to take pictures of these next few frames." We all bring up our phones, cameras at the ready. "I will hold up some papers with bank names, account numbers, passwords, and PIN numbers. All the cards are in the museum lockbox, they are in Fate's name. I was so lucky to have her parents around for as long as I did. The use of their magic has really made hiding things in Fate's name so much easier." My jaw drops at that, but I can't stop watching this train wreck. "In that locker you will find a spray bottle. Her parents spelled it so that when you spray it on yourself, no one will be able to tell that you are not Fate. The effects only last for a couple hours, but that should be plenty of time for you to transfer things over to you. Here you go babe, I love you more than anything."

We all snap pictures as he holds up three separate sheets of information. I will pass all this right along to Memré. She should have no problem getting these transferred as well. The video ends after the last sheet and one more I love you, Amalia. I am sick of her already.

"Guess we are going on a scavenger hunt really soon. What a jerk he is, I mean the audacity on him. Wow."

Ajah says, "Man, I had no idea a guy could be that shady. I mean, damn. Most guys are shady, but he took it there."

I laugh, "He did, didn't he? He is a piece of work, all right. Ok. Let's watch the last one and then I want to get out of here. I don't know what Marina has planned for dinner tonight, but I am eager to try her cooking."

Ajah pops in the last one and Natasha hits play. She looks pensive, but I will ask her later. The video plays and here is Charlie once again. "Amalia Terner, my love, I hope this video finds you well. If you are seeing it, I can only guess that either you used that little bit of spray I left you with to use in an emergency or Fate did the right thing," I snort at that line, he wouldn't know the right thing if it walked up and slapped his face off. "And gave you the videos meant for you without watching them. Or perhaps she died and you have just taken over her life. Get everything you can out of her name before they find her body and get yourself out of there. Hire someone to go in and deep clean the house to remove any DNA or finger prints you might leave behind. I highly advise you to take another name and leave the country, go to somewhere that won't send you back here if the US wants to try you for something.

Do not trust her sister, she is greedy and conniving. She has some way of knowing things," Natasha and I exchange a look at this, "that she shouldn't know. I don't know how she does it, but it happens and I never could find any bugs in the house. Get yourself away from these people love, they are crazy and awful and someone as good as you should never have to deal with them. I will always love you, Amalia, always."

My eyes roll involuntarily at that last line. The bit about Pru confirms my fear that we will have to take steps to stop her from her depravities. "Ok, that is the last of them. I want to take these with us, so we can go treasure hunting. See what else my darling dead husband left for his mistress, Amalia Terner. I guess now that we have a name that will make it easier to track her down should we need to." As I have been talking Natasha collected the disk from the player and set the remote on top, I put the lid back on the box and set the tissue box near it, Ajah moved the trash bin to a corner. Natasha hands me the disk and I slip it back into a sleeve, collect the other three and drop them in my purse. We leave the room and head out front, I thank Beth for the tissues and wave to Benjamin as I cross the waiting area. He waves back and says, "Call if you need anything!"

I tell him I will and we get ourselves out of there and on the way home.

$\maltese$ *9* $\maltese$

We arrive back at the house and it seems like everyone is on high alert, all four of my other body guards run out to escort us from the car. Ajah falls in, taking up the rear guard, though none of us have any clue what exactly is going on. Inside the house they shut the door and throw the locks, ushering Natasha and I upstairs to the office. I am quickly growing tired of this nonsense, I can smell what Marina is cooking and I want it. In my office with the blinds pulled shut I throw my purse down on the desk and looking directly at Steve I say, "You have about 10 seconds to share some information before I lose my whole temper. The day has been long and I have no patience for games."

Steve looks very uncomfortable as Ajah snickers behind him. Pulling at his collar he says, "Well, about an hour after you sent us all that text Pru showed up here." My eyes go wide at that, "She was looking for you, said she missed you. When we told her you weren't here and we didn't know when you would be back, we felt her trying to break through that spell you and Natasha did before you left. Man, am I glad you did that. Will that work on any mind reader?" I nod and motion for him to go on, "Well, when she couldn't get into my mind or Brad's she went crazy. She kicked me in the shin and started screaming about dirty witches always hiding things, and how her son would have everything he always deserved and how dare Fate play these games. It was insane all the things she was screaming. Then she said she would be back and that you better be ready to see her."

My jaw is hanging open at this point, "What? She has lost her ever-lovin' mind. She might actually need treatment, her son died. Like, he died at birth. The sweet little boy never even really took a breath. It was years ago, I don't understand this at all. Natasha, I think maybe now is the time."

She looks as stricken as I feel when she says, "I think you are right. We need to get this done. She can't be allowed to run rampant and possibly do damage to people."

Steve pales, "Damage? She could have done damage to my brain?"

I look at Natasha and back at him, "Well, yes. Normally that wouldn't be a worry, but right now with how unhinged her behavior is, she may not be fully in control of herself or her abilities."

He runs a hand through his hair, "Fuck. There are more of these types out there? Fate, Natasha; I don't know how to thank you for putting that spell on my brain, but let me know if you come up with something."

I smile, "No need. We are going to step into the other side of my office and stop Pru. Where is Devon?"

"He is in his office with Billy, they said they would stay there for the time being as they were working anyway."

"Ah, I see. One of you will need to come over here to this side and pay attention to everyone left over here, we won't be able to hear you." Ajah nods and walks over to stand with Natasha and I, we all clasp hands and walk through the barrier. After we are through, I see that Ajah has turned back and appears to be signing to Steve, who is signing back. The conversation seems pretty fierce, so I wait for them to finish. "What was that about?"

"Oh, he doesn't like that I volunteer so much. But he can stick it."

I laugh, "I see, and I am guessing that he didn't want us to be let in on that." Steve is glaring at Ajah through the barrier. She laughs, crosses her arms and says, "Nope. He sure didn't. He also doesn't want you to know that this whole mind reading thing makes him want to wet himself, it scares him so bad."

"Aw, well, we will not mention that to him ever. No one should be made fun of for their fears. Well, unless they are not really fears but just the word fear being used to get away with being an awful person. Ok, Natasha, you got that spell pulled up? We need to get this done, I want whatever Marina is cooking."

Natasha doesn't even look up, "Yes. Got it right here. Do we have anything of hers?"

I think about it, and I do. I need to go to my bedroom. All my things are still mostly stacked in the closet. There is a memory book in there. When Pru and I were little, I was making this book, and I wanted to have a piece of her hair in it, I don't know why I wanted it then but I am glad I have it now.

"I do, let me go to my bedroom and get it out." I step through the barrier, "I need to get something from my room, you can walk with me or get out of the way." Brad straightens from the wall he has been leaning against, "I'll go." I nod and stroll out down the hall with Brad behind me. I enter the closet and realize I don't know which box it is in. "Going to be a few minutes here Brad. I have to find the book." He peeks in the closet and sees the five boxes sitting on the floor. "Want some help?"

I shrug, "Sure. We are looking for a memory book. You start with that box and I got this one."

He nods and opens it up, rifling through the items inside as he says, "So I was listening earlier when Gibbs was talking. That chick is your sister? And she is doing this kind of stuff to you?"

I shrug a shoulder and frown, "Yeah. It isn't the kind of thing I ever expected from her. But I didn't know they adopted me either. Maybe that makes a difference."

"Not where I come from, no ma'am. Family sticks to family and we don't hurt anyone on purpose. Accidents happen sometimes when we play too much. But we take care of each other. I can't imagine what my family would do if one of us behaved like that."

I nod as I abandon the box I just finished and open the next, "Yeah. I thought that was what our family was like, but now... Well, those illusions have been ripped away like the proverbial band-aid very recently. Found it!"

I grab the book out of the box and flip through the pages till I come to the envelope marked Prudence; I flip open the flap and there is my prize. Hair from my sister's head cut by me years ago. I close the flap and the book, Brad and I head back to the office. I step into the witching area and show Natasha my prize. Ajah says, "Hey, the guys say Memré is here, you want her up here?"

"Oh! Yes! Let me know when she gets in the room, I will bring her through."

We carefully take a portion of the hair and drop it into the small cauldron that Natasha prepared while I was out of the room. The cauldron has some sort of viscous liquid in it that smells heavily of mugwort and she stirs the hair into it with a small glass rod. That done, she puts the rod off to the side and picks up the cauldron. Turning to me she says, "From what I read this will feel like it is burning the hell out of us, but it won't actually burn us physically. Apparently it is one of the safeguards from the Goddess, so that this isn't done lightly. Also, if we were doing this for revenge or something petty, it would immediately rebound on us and take our power away. The spell mentions too that for those doing this for all the right reasons, there is no protection possible for the one they cast upon. This spell is handed down by the Goddess Persephone herself."

"Well, ok then. No pressure."

Natasha nods, "Link your fingers with mine so we are both supporting the cauldron," I thread my fingers through hers, the weight of the pot supported now by our linked hands, "Ajah, can you hold the book—"

"Here she is."

I look at Natasha, "Hang on, let's get her in here. She can hold the book." Un-linking our hands, I walk over and grab Memré's hand, pulling her through, "Great timing. Come on over here. We need you to hold the book while we bind Pru."

"What the hell? I mean, I will, because of the messages earlier and the goons on high alert out there, not to mention the fact that Pru is in your front yard shrieking… But you got some explaining to do real soon."

Threading my fingers back through Natasha's I nod, "Sure thing. Let's get this show on the road. Grab that book and hold it so we can see the spell."

Memré grabs the book and is quickly standing next to us. "On three Natasha, one, two, three."

We recite the verse together:

A gift of powers
Maintain the balance
Abuse of others
No second chance
Power you may not recover
Persephone, for your judgment I call
For the safety of all

As we recite the words to the spell, the liquid in the pot begins to glow and bubble. The heat coming from the pot is intense, and it feels like the flesh is melting off my fingers. Memré looks on in amazement as the stuff in the cauldron vaporizes and tears stream down our face from the pain. As the last words to the spell fall from our lips, the pain disappears like it never was. We nearly drop the cauldron in shock. I catch it and Natasha takes it from me, setting it on the table. As Memré sets the book down, Ajah says, "Uh, guys. Steve says we should step out and hear this."

We exchange a look and all clasp hands, stepping out of my magical space together so we can hear exactly what Steve is talking about. My sister is outside my office screaming at the top of her lungs. She has a whole diatribe going about how evil I am and how our parents were right to set her to watching me. She says she will never forgive me for taking her powers from her. I can't even blame her for that.

I go to the window and open it up. Sticking my head out I holler down to Pru, "Would you like to come in and talk about this or you just want to stand out on my lawn and scream?"

Pru's mouth snaps shut and she gives me the finger. I laugh and she stomps off to her car, gets in and leaves. I pull my head in. As I shut the window I tell everyone, "I guess she didn't want to talk. So, how about we cast that spell on Memré real quick Natasha, so she doesn't have to worry about being mind-raped either?"

Memré looks over at me, "What the fuck is going on here?"

Steve chimes in, "Just let them do the spell. You won't regret it. I promise."

Memré's jaw drops, "What? Why would he say that? Did Pru? Oh, no…"

I nod, "She did. If we hadn't set the spell on them before we left the house today… I don't want to think about what could have happened."

"Oh Sweet Jeebus. Ok. Get that spell on me now, then we get food right? Whatever is cooking down there, I would kill to get some."

We quickly take Memré back through the barrier and cast the spell on her. It takes a lot less time to cast it on one person than on many. Within five minutes we are all downstairs loitering in the dining room. Devon and Billy joined us as we walked out of the office, so we walked down arm in arm.

Not too long after we all sat down, Marina and her helpers came out with trays of food and it is all so fragrant. Once all the dishes are on the table Sherri takes the trays back to the kitchen while Marina and Nicki sit down and fill their plates. Once she comes back, everyone is silent for a time with the eating. Once the initial rush is over Memré is the one to break the silence saying, "Ok Lucy, want to start with the explanations or what?"

The whole table turned to look at me, not uncomfortable at all…

"Um, yeah. So my sister, she is a mind reader. For years she has beaten her way into my mind and spied on everything I have ever done. I thought it was a sister thing. I didn't like it, but I felt it was something we would work out, eventually."

Memré shakes her head, "Oh honey, that is horrible. Your parents never knew?"

"Well, actually, it was their idea." I watch Memré's jaw drop and snap shut, "Oh yeah, surprise. I was adopted too. They decided after they finally conceived a child within months of adopting me, I must be evil. So they tried to bind my powers. That didn't work out so great. Then Pru's powers came in and they just taught her that it was her right to monitor the thoughts of others, mine especially." I can feel the pity from the entire table and it is really not the most comfortable thing I have ever experienced. "I didn't know about any of this really until recently. But as Pru has been nastier with the mind-raping lately, I decided I would talk to Griselda about it, see if there was a spell to keep her out without having to fight her for possession of my mind. She was the one that told us about my being adopted, took the glamour off of me and gave me the spells we used tonight. You know, I just realized, I haven't needed my glasses since she took the glamour off... Interesting. Today I went to watch the videos that Charlie left for me and Fake Fate, whose actual name is Amalia Terner. Well, he had a lot to say about Pru. Pru knew about everything he was doing. She was an accomplice at the least, just by helping keep me in the dark. At worst, she seemed to be aiding and encouraging him, the way my parents also did before they died. He told Amalia, in one of the videos, to watch out for Pru because she 'could know things she shouldn't be able to know' and that was when I decided enough was enough. It was time to do what Griselda had told me I had to do. Then when I got home, everyone was in an uproar over the behavior Pru had displayed when she came by to see me. And then she showed up again to screech in the front yard. She flipped me off when she left, ha."

Memré had stopped eating while I was telling the story, stunned at the betrayal by Pru. She was part of our little family, but now it seems like she was playing us all. I can imagine how she is feeling, I have been there for a few days now. "You ok Memré?"

"Yes, I am fine. It is just appalling that she would do this. And your parents! I mean damn, I noticed the drastic change in your appearance and I planned to ask about it when it was just us girls but I never imagined that they would do something so heinous as to strip a part of who you are from you, and to attempt to strip the magic that is part of your very soul from you just because you exist? It might take a minute or five to wrap my head around this." She shakes her head, mumbling, "She worked with Charlie against her own sister? How could she do that?"

We all go back to eating, silent again and somber at this point. The revelations of how deep the betrayal by Pru and my parents really goes have affected everyone. The faces looking back at me are somber and reflect a deep sympathy I would have thought to get from my sister for the betrayal of a friend.

"But wait, I forgot, there's more! Charlie hid a lot more money in various places. Accounts, which we now have all the pertinent information for getting into and some of it in spots around the city. So we need to go on a treasure hunt sometime soon." Looking around the table, I see dropped jaws and smirks. Natasha and Ajah are the ones smirking while everyone else is stunned.

Brad finally speaks, "If we find it, do we get a raise?"

The entire table breaks out in laughter, I soak up the noise of happiness. It is music to my soul. I could listen to the laughter of friends, new and old, for hours. I feel a little of what cracked in my heart healing just a little as the laughter dies down. This is what family should be like. The one I had may have been all I knew, but it was never this good. Now I know why.

Looking at the people sitting at our table, I know that family isn't always who you are born with and sometimes it isn't who you think it is. But when you find them, find those people that make you feel accepted and loved just as you are, darkness and all; those people are your family and truly the ones worth fighting beside. My life is strange and hectic and really a lot more dangerous lately, but I wouldn't trade it for anything.

"Yes Brad, everyone will get a raise." I smile at him and the rest of the table. Devon reaches over and taking my hand he draws it to his lips, kissing my knuckles. He murmurs against my knuckles, "You are a goddess and I am so lucky to be a part of your life." I blush, hearing a few snickers come from other parts of the table.

Looking toward Memré, I ask her, "How do you feel about coming to work for me?"

She finishes chewing and swallowing before saying, "Heh, I feel it is going to be expensive. But it looks like you might be able to afford it. What did you have in mind?"

"I feel like I need some in house internet security and computer techs. I think you are best for the job. My thoughts were that I could pull you away from freelancing by offering a challenge, a clean slate for that challenge, and a salary commensurate to what you make now plus a little. No hourly work requirements, just that you stay on top of things. Because I am not hiring people to occupy a space. You would also have free rein to hire a team, or fire them as need be. What do you think about that?"

"That sounds great but I have projects running through the end of the year that I can't just walk away from. Can you wait that long or nah?"

"Hmmm, can you start the work in your spare time, at full pay rate? We have time to start things rolling slowly and build on in incremental bits. Right now we have found our building and have a rough framework on what we want to do, but not much more. So if you start to put together an idea of how the computer system will work, what software we will use, what computers, etc.; that would be great. I plan to open sometime next year, probably. Depending on what obstacles I run into. I have already hired my realtor on retainer, she is making all her money off me at this point because that is what she has time for with all my properties. I am thinking about tapping into Benjamin, seeing if I can lure him away to be the head lawyer for the foundation. Because for all that you all have the skill sets I need in this venture the thing you all have in colossal amounts and which is the most important to me, is loyalty. I can trust you all to have all of our best interests at heart, and that is more important to me than any skill set."

"Gosh. Put that way how could I refuse? Besides, I am a little bored with work, anyway. The challenge is gone. This might offer a lasting challenge, or maybe I can take minor charity jobs for fun."

"Ha! There you go! I am so glad you are going to work with us! I will feel so much more secure and I can only imagine how much fun you are going to have building a whole new system."

❧

Devon

❧

Walking into the parlor, I close the door behind me and turn to face all the bodyguards and Billy.

"I know you are all wondering why I have called you in here, and it is all about Fate." I shove my hands in my pockets and begin to pace the room, "In this life she seems to be very brave but also less concerned with her own safety than she ever has been. Charles has been the one to kill her in most of her previous incarnations, and he knows where she is now. He has already tried to take her out on many occasions and has recently decided that he is in love with her this time around. I can't tell if Fate just isn't taking this very seriously, or she just isn't worried, but I am. This is where you come in. The less Charles knows about you, the better. If he thinks you are human and just employees, part of her entourage, he will underestimate you." I see Ajah smirking, I need to talk to her to find out what that is about. "So keep your appearances as human as possible. Less visibly sniffing the air. Less growling. Try to look like a regular employee or friend." Ajah is full on grinning now at something behind me, I turn and see Natasha standing in the doorway, hand still on the knob. Her jaw is dropped, and it snaps shut as I see her. She smiles slowly, "Oh, I am telling Fate about this. Bad Devon, I hope you get a spanking." She laughs as she closes the door and I hear her heels clicking off into the distance. I rub my forehead with one hand as the shifters make excuses to be anywhere else. I don't even bother looking up as they leave. Billy pats me on the back as he passes by, "It was a nice try. But not your best move ever. You'll probably survive the night though." He laughs as he walks away.

I am in so much trouble.

❈   10   ❈

I see Natasha come in the office through the mirror I hung up in front of my workstation. I set markers in the pages and walk over, extending my hand through the barrier to bring her in. "We should probably look into some way of changing this or maybe just take it down and put up a whole other one." Natasha grins, "You think? We could do that in a little bit. For now, I have so much news."

I raise a brow at her, "Oh really?"

That grin just got wider, "Yes, really. I was checking rooms to figure out where I left my phone. I opened the parlor door and dear old Devon was giving the bodyguards a speech. Wanna know what it was about?"

My eyes roll, I just know this is going to be ridiculous. Couple steps back and I sit in the chair, "Ok. Spill the tea,

I know he must have done something dumb for you to be this entertained."

"Of course he did. He didn't realize I was there, but Ajah did. He was explaining to them how you aren't cautious enough with yourself and with Charles running around they need to be really watching out for you. He realized I was there before he got to telling them to put your safety above everything else. I told him I would tell you. He was rubbing his forehead when I left."

"Uggghghghghgh. I know his heart is in the right place, but leashing me isn't the way to go about this. We are going to have a nice loud conversation about this later. Don't worry, I will put an air shield around the room to keep the sound from bleeding into the rest of the house."

"Well, spoil my fun, why don't you. I get it though, and it should be like that. I actually really agree that you should be turned now. Yesterday. Two weeks ago. I don't get his hold out. I have actually been thinking about coming over to the dark side. Plenty of vampires have offered, but I didn't want to if I wasn't going to have one of my long-term friends with me."

Leaning forward, I ask her, "Serious? Really? That would be the best thing ever! I would love to know I have one of my girls with me for the long run. I would never ask you to do it, but if you decide you want to, it would thrill me. And now that we have cleared that up," I watch suspicion flit across her face at my change in tone, "What is going on with you and Billy? I am sensing some tension…"

Natasha's cheeks light up and I grin while she says, "Well, we might have kissed outside the restaurant and maybe both of us liked it really a lot. The kiss was actually how we lost Amalia. We were both so into it that when we surfaced for air, she was long gone."

"Scandalous! I love it. I thought you two would get to that conclusion, eventually. What are you going to do about it now?"

"I don't know. I mean, what if we try it and it doesn't work? I don't date in our circle because I didn't want to cause any complications." Natasha actually seems concerned about this and I put away the grin, "Oh honey, vampires aren't really your usual guy. I mean, Charles is obviously an exception, but the majority of them have been dealing with these things for hundreds of years. Plus, if you date another vampire and it doesn't work out they can't hate each other forever. They have learned how to get past these things and you will too, or you already know how and it will just be so much easier. I mean, you have already dated vampires, right?"

"Yeah."

"Are you still friends with them? Still cool even though you aren't together anymore?"

"Yeah, every one of them actually."

I shrug, "See? It will be no problem, and it could be really great. Give it a shot. If you choose, no pressure. I am good either way. Though you are my family, even before him. So I will take your side always. And if you are wrong, I will give you shit later."

She laughs at my sentiment and comes over to hug me, "I couldn't ask for a better friend than you Fate. You're the best."

"Good, now that that is settled, let's get to work. We have spells to fix and spells to catalogue. Mostly the cataloguing, I feel like we might find a spell that would be better for the job somewhere in all this."

Natasha sits at the table and opens her laptop and I begin to read off the spell titles and authors. We work companionably like this until nearly midnight, when Devon comes to remind me that I had planned to go look at the new building tomorrow. We close up shop because I really do want to see this place. I have complete faith that Natasha and Billy chose the perfect place to house the foundation. Tomorrow is going to be the best day ever! All my friends with me and a brand new building to house a foundation for magical people.

❧ 11 ☙

F

ate

Maggie dropped off the keys and codes for the buildings this morning before I was anything resembling awake. I thought I was going to have a long talk with Devon about why he won't just turn me already last night. As it turns out I was exhausted and I barely made it to the bed before I fell asleep. I know I don't have time today; he is leaving shortly to see his accountant. I will be out of here as soon as I can get myself together. As great as this house is, I wonder if maybe we should just buy our own place. One that is close to the right size before we do anything to it. I could buy it, or he could, or we could go in half. Actually, I think I will buy it as a surprise. I will call Maggie later and see what she can find me.

Coffee, must have coffee first.

DEVON

As I slide into the seat of my Audi Billy says, "My friend. Why are we avoiding Fate? I will go where you go and I will keep your secrets, but I need to know why."

I start the engine and pull out of the drive, taking a left to head toward the more crowded areas. Billy is silent, but I know he won't let this go. I have to figure out what to say to him without telling him I don't want to risk her dying if I or someone else kills Charles. I can't reveal that I am afraid of Charles dying because I don't want to die. And what if I am killed? I should have never mentioned it to her! But she would have remembered eventually, anyway. One more thing I can lay at Charles' door. My sense of smell is almost nonexistent, but that close I could smell Charles on the guy that tried to mug Fate. I don't know if he planned to kill her that night or not. Billy reaches over and flicks my ear, "Ow! What did you do that for?" He scowls at me, "I did it because you haven't answered my question yet. Maybe you answered it in your head, but it doesn't count until I hear the words."

"Oh, yeah…" Think fast, Kordell. "I am just not ready for her to change yet. Becoming a vampire changes a person, and I only just found her. I know I should respect her wishes, and I will. I just need to enjoy some time with her first. I have never seen her this age, and it is amazing. She is gorgeous, talented, mouthy, and a little broken admittedly. But she is so much more for having had all these experiences, and I just want to savor it a little longer."

Billy licks his lips and I know he has got things to say. "Listen, I get that. But I don't think this is about you. Especially since you haven't told her any of that. You ride her about being more safe and taking precautions and taking bodyguards with her, but you won't grant her the one thing she has actually asked for in all of this. Nor will you give her the ok for someone else to do it in your place. You are being incredibly selfish and you should be ashamed."

I wish I could tell him, but that is a weakness to that could be exploited and what if one day he is my enemy? No. Better to keep my own counsel in this matter. "I know this is a selfish indulgence, but it is what I need right now. And I hate the idea of anyone else drinking from her. I feel insane with rage over the idea."

"Let me put this in terms you can easily understand. Stupid. Selfish. Ridiculous. And, this is going to blow up in your face. I don't know how, but I feel it in my bones. Something is coming and if you haven't turned her by then, it's gonna be a real bad day my friend."

"What is coming? What do you know? Tell me!"

"I don't know anything. Slow down, asshole. You can afford the ticket, but time in jail will be really shitty for you. It is just a feeling. Something big is coming, and it is going to change everything if she is still only a witch. That's another thing, you are preventing her from a whole other line of defense! Why? Why not suck it up and do the right thing?"

"I just can't yet, ok?"

"No. It isn't ok. But I suppose it will have to do. I am warning you though, if she comes to me and asks me to turn her, I will. In a heartbeat."

"You wouldn't!"

"Bet. I won't unless she asks. But if she asks, it will be done. Did you know Natasha is going to become one as well?"

"What? When was that decided? Why didn't anyone tell me?"

"A few reasons. One, it isn't your business what she does. Two, she has her own vampire connections and doesn't have to rely on you. Which is a thing you may want to keep in mind as you continue to deny Fate her turning. Three, it isn't officially decided yet. I think she is waiting for Fate."

"Oh."

Fate

The buildings aren't far away from the house, but really nothing seems very far away in a city. At least, not to me. Once I visited a cousin that lived pretty far out from a small town and even farther from the closest city center. It was bananas. I don't want to drive an hour or so to get into the area I need to be in to get to the place I need to go. Just no way.

Oh wow. These buildings are perfect! It is like a little compound of buildings. Natasha has the keys, and she walks around unlocking doors, Steve walks with her while the other four walk with me, slowly exploring the buildings. They told me there are eight buildings total. The first one holds multiple offices and a small reception area. The second and third are also multiple office type areas. The fourth one seems to be for group meetings while the fifth building square in the middle is one large office. Building number 6 is a kitchen/lunch area. Buildings seven and eight are connected by a long hall between them and a playground that both buildings open into from the interior walls. I am walking out of building four when something whizzes past my face and I smell the acrid scent of gunpowder. John snatches me back into the building and half drags me into the bathrooms, he shoves me toward the stalls and I stop. "You do know I am magic and completely capable of aiding in my defense, right?" He looks down, "Um, I forgot." I shake my head at him. "How about we go back out but with a little magical bullet-proof vest? Over us and everyone else." He nods and I tell him, "Hang on just a moment." I quickly weave air so that it forms a shield around each of us from head to toe while still allowing for full range movement and breathing. I give him a thumbs up and he runs out the door with me not far behind. We can hear shots being fired, John motions for me to get against the wall as he pulls his own gun and sees what he can see through the open door. "I see Steve and Natasha, they are in the next building over. The shots seem to be being fired from the building at the end with the playground. I can't see Ajah, Brad, or Owen. They are probably trying to circle around and get behind her." A shot hits the doorway of the building we are hiding in and fragments fly, some hitting John. "This shield thing is great. How long can you hold this together?"

"Um, indefinitely? I just put it together. Air does the rest. I don't know that it would ever dissipate if I didn't ask it to do so."

He turns to look at me, "What? Would anyone else be able to do anything about it?"

Just then we hear the sound of an enormous cat in a fight. The sound grows to include wolves and a bear, John begins to whimper a little and I tell him, "Go, I am safe enough here. I promise I won't leave the building."

"Promise?"

"Yes. Go before I change my mind. They might need help."

I slide down the wall and sit on the floor. My bones might not appreciate it later, but right now I just really want to sit. I can't help but stare toward the sound of the fight, which only seems to have intensified. Imagine my surprise when Charles creeps into the building. He doesn't see me at first and so I grab air to create a wall around myself and keep him from touching me. I slowly stand as he spots me. He walks over, looking all smug until he walks face first into my wall.

"Epic face plant Charles. What are you doing here? Is all this your doing? Did you set up someone to shoot at us so you could get me alone? Because really, that is incredibly lame."

Charles stops inspecting my wall for holes or gaps and focuses on me. "No, Fate darling, I did not set this up. The shooting is Maude, your lover's old housekeeper. And the woman hired to murder you by your dead husband. What kind of relationship did the two of you have? You were still visiting his grave when I first saw you, and he had hired someone to kill you. Doesn't seem like the healthiest of relationships. Maybe you should consider that your current relationship isn't the healthiest either."

I lean against the wall and cross my arms, "Interesting tactic, Charles. What are you doing here? Are you stalking me? Why would you stalk me? We have nothing in common. Last I saw you, weren't you blowing across a field like a tumbleweed?"

His lips turn down and his eyes narrow, "Yes, I was. With a rather nasty burn on my arm at that. But I forgive you." He follows the air wall to where it meets with the stone of the building and tries to work his fingers under what he perceives to be an edge. It isn't but I make it feel like it is covered in a thousand tiny needles anyway. "OW! You little minx! Naughty, Naughty. Won't you come out here and let's talk about your punishment?"

"I think I will wait in here. I am cozy and I do believe that I am not hearing the sounds of fighting anymore. I would say it limits your time before my bodyguards come back in here and turn you into zoo food."

He cocks his head to one side and draws his brows down, "Zoo food?" He shakes his head and holds his hand out toward me, "Come Fate, we should leave." I hear growls and I start to laugh.

Two wolves, a bear, and two tigers stalk into the room. "Charles, I would leave now if I were you. They sound unhappy."

He looks between me and the animals advancing on him, "But Fate, won't you help me love?"

"Ugh, you don't get to call me that. GO AWAY CHARLES."

The growls intensify and the shifters are spreading out to block all the exits. This is certainly going to solve a problem for me. I hear the sound of breaking glass and I look up to see Charles gone and one of my windows trashed. Frame and all. Thank Goddess I can find someone in the magical community to fix this so I can just be honest with them about the cause of the damage. I ask them, "Is it okay to drop my shield now, guys?" The wolves look at each other and one of the tigers nods at me. They drift one at a time into the bathroom hallway to change, shifting back to their human forms. I wonder, where do shifter clothes go when they shift? Brad, one of the tigers, is first to change. I ask him, "Where are Steve and Natasha?" He dips his head toward the neighboring building, "They are over there. I think she got clipped by a bullet," my face must have shown how I felt about that because he held up his hands, "It was nothing serious! I promise! But he wouldn't have been able to do much to it till the shooting stopped, and then he would have wanted to clean it properly before doing anything else. Just hang out for a minute. The woman that was shooting at us got away. She had the whole damn roof booby trapped. That was what most of the fight was, just trying to get to her. Ajah got to her first, knocked her gun out of her hand, and they fought a little. Before we could all get to her, the crazy bitch jumped off the building! Sailed right off and into the brush back there. Not the brightest thing ever, but also not the dumbest as she did get away."

About that time Natasha limps into the building, followed by Steve. I rush over, grabbing her in a hug that she returns, "I am so glad you are ok! You are ok, aren't you? Why are you limping? Let me see! Do you need anything?" I release her and step back to look at the leg she was favoring. There is an ace bandage wrapped around it over some gauze pads, it doesn't look terrible. But it probably sucks. I look up to find Natasha watching me, her eyes crinkled and a smile playing across her lips. "Too much, huh?"

She laughs, "A little, but not bad overall. It really is fine. Just makes walking uncomfortable. I have done worse to myself having sex." Ajah, walking out of the hall just in time to hear the last sentence laughs her head off. I think that is our cue to go home.

13

I am so tired. Today has been such a long day! It did not get better when we got home. Billy and Devon were already here, and Billy got real mad about missing today after he saw Natasha's leg. In fact, I think I need to talk to Devon about some of the things he said. He called Devon some names that I would be interested to know the reason for their usage.

The argument was brief, but Billy seemed to be holding back from things he truly wanted to say. I get into bed thinking we are going to talk first, but Devon has other plans. He is over me as soon as I lay down, kissing my neck and asking me if I would make love to him. How am I going to say no, I want to talk with him kissing my neck like that? Then he scrapes the skin ever so lightly with his eye teeth and a shiver goes through my entire body.

Panting, I whisper, "Yes Devon, please Devon, take me Devon…" in his ear. He freezes in place as I whisper in his ear, "I need it, Devon." He growls and snatches the blankets off me, pressing his body against mine he encircles me with his arms and rolls so I am now on top of him. I bring my knees up to straddle him, feeling his velvety hardness press against my most sensitive areas. I lift my torso so I can look down at him. Taking his hands, I put them on my hips and hold them in place for now.

Rocking my pelvis forward a little, I press the head of his member into my swollen nub before easing the pressure and sliding forward to let his cock rise a bit. I wiggle my hips, adjusting till he lines up with my soaking wet entrance. Slowly, a millimeter at a time, I slide his full length into me. He tries to thrust the rest in about halfway thru but I lift up until he is only barely touching, "No darling, you put me on top and now I get to play. Lay still and let me torment you." He moans as I begin to rock my hips, still just barely touching the head with my hot folds. He begins to pant and I ask him softly, "Will you lay still while I torture you until you come for me, my sweet Devon?"

"Yes, yes, anything you want." He growls as I dip my core down to cover the head and rock my hips there. His agreement given, I slam down to the hilt once before lifting back up to encase only the tip. He shouts and grips my hips as I swirl his member in my fiery core.

"Oh God, oh yes, oh Fate." He says over and over as I lean forward allowing him access to my breasts as I ride him hard and fast. He takes one hand off my hip and slips a finger between us, putting pressure on my nub and I ride him faster and harder till we both explode into the most intense pequeña muerte I have ever experienced, our bodies vibrating so intensely it almost becomes pain before the spasms recede. I lower my torso down so I am pressed against him. We lay unmoving for a time, too sensitive to even disengage.

Our breathing slowly returns to normal and I roll off to one side as slow as I can. Even still, the friction sends shivers through the both of us. Laying there trying to catch the little pieces left of my soul after it shattered with the searing pleasure of that orgasm, I remember that I wanted to talk to him about turning me. I roll onto my side and look down into his eyes; they glitter a little in the darkness. "Devon," I say as I work to distract him by tracing lazy circles on his chest, "why won't you turn me? I feel like time is running out and we need to get this done, but you seem hesitant to do it. Why?"

"Because I'm afraid you'll die."

"What?" My hand on his chest jerks to a halt and I lean closer, "Say that again?"

"I'm afraid you'll die if I turn you now. You have barely gotten to live in most of your lives, I don't want to be the reason why your life is ended permanently." He turns to look directly at me, "There is no reincarnation for vampires. We get one shot and if we screw it up and die early, that is just too bad for us."

"Wait, I don't get it. So you are afraid I will die because vampires only get one shot at this thing we call life?"

He sighs, "No. I'm afraid you will die if I turn you and then Charles dies."

"What?" I sit up facing him with my legs crossed. Probably not the sexiest position ever, so I tug a corner of the blanket over my lap. "I need further explanation. You are speaking cryptically and I don't care for it at all, mister. Spit it all out now. Tell me the entire issue in very clear language that even an older child would understand."

He sits up and leans himself against the headboard, "As far as I know, when a vampire's maker is killed, so too dies his line. So if Charles dies then I die and if you are turned by me, so do you."

"I don't know. That doesn't make a lot of sense. I mean, I know you all are a long-lived race, but if the whole damn line died with one of the elders... Well, you all were pretty violent to begin with, wouldn't the whole species have come close enough to extinction many times from murder and death by accident or human? How do you know these things are true?"

"I am a vampire Fate."

I can't even help the eye roll here, "Yes. You are, not that I had noticed or anything. Do you get a knowledge infusion with the turning? Do you instantly know certain things once you turn? How did you gain this knowledge?" I gasp as a thought occurs to me, "You don't know, do you? That's why you were researching vampires when you came to the library! Devon, why didn't you just ask a friend?"

He looks away, "The vampire sire is supposed to tell the fledgling the things they are supposed to know. Charles turned me for spite, he barely told me anything. What he did tell me is that you can't trust vampires, the politics and honor will get you every time. I am guessing really about the sire usually teaching the ones they turn. Based on things I heard."

"Oh Devon," I cup his cheek with my hand, "the only vampire you know for sure that you can't trust is Charles. I need to spend some time with Billy, and I strongly advise that you come clean with him. Or at least sit in with us while we talk. I feel like there are things we should both know about being a vampire, but you especially."

"I can't ask about things, Fate. I can't even appear to be trying to figure things out by overhearing. It would cause me to lose status in the vampire world."

"What does that mean? Lose status? What are the consequences of losing status in your world? Is it like being short? Do you not get to ride all the rides? What happens?

Because really, if it is just some snotty fucker looking down on you, who cares?"

"It is a little more some snotty fucker looking down on me, the whole vampire community would after word got around."

"Wait, so even your friends would report on that? Even though your sire severely handicapped you in regards to knowledge?"

"That is what I have seen so far, yes."

"So there are others that have had sires that didn't fulfill their duty?"

"Uh. No, not per se..."

"Not per se? Explain."

"Well, I have never heard of any in my particular situation."

"Then you don't know that is what would happen. Listen, someone is going to turn me really soon. I have too many people trying to kill me not to take advantage of any leg up on them that I can grab. My life is on the line here and while I understand that you have concerns about what happens if you kill Charles, well, not everyone was sired by Charles. And I do know from my talk with those past witches that if one of us is permanently out of the rebirth cycle, the bond will break and the one left will be free to live without the longing. So, if you turn me, one of us dies, and you are right about not coming back; well, the other one can go on. With a normal grieving period. As opposed to what you went through every time I died."

He is silent for a long time, and I wait while he turns things over in his head. I hear him move in the dark of our bedroom. He touches his forehead to mine and says, "Interview Billy. Find out the things we need to know, and whatever else you want to put in the book. I will accept whatever you find out. Will that satisfy you?"

"Not as much as it would if you would set aside the pride that keeps you from telling your friend the truth and just talking to him, but it'll do. For now."

I SHOULD HAVE GONE TO SLEEP WHEN HE DID, BUT I AM awake now. Maybe I could put this time to good use? Well, I want to talk to the witches again, see if they know anything more about our situation. I don't know if I am in contact with people and I am jumping time a bit or if they are some sort of spell with limited access to knowledge… I should ask. That settles it.

A few minutes later I am walking the halls in my mind, seeking the book I used to see them last time. There it is! I open the book and suddenly am seated in a room with three other witches, none look surprised to see me. They do however request that I put on clothing… I focus on wearing clothing, hoping I am not manifesting clothing on my corporeal body as well. Clothing on, I apologize to them, "I was in my bed not sleeping. I forgot that I was not wearing clothing and that would be reflected in my meditative state unless I corrected it. I am so sorry."

The ladies laugh and tease a little, but they don't dwell on it so I get to my questions. "I don't know how long I will be able to stay here ladies, but I have some questions, if you would be willing to answer them?"

Kate answers me, "Yes, we are happy to answer your questions. But before that, we need to turn you to your task. You were meant to be talking with the families and collecting the knowledge of the witches, and you have a good start, that's sure. But there is more yet to be done. You must get in contact with the families, each of the 13. You should know, they were meant to have been collecting the spells of the other families and it should have spiraled out to encompass as many families as possible. It has not, and that is in part because there was no one to guide them. Witches being people too, they are susceptible to some of the same foibles as humans. You must get them back on track. Additionally, please send our thanks to Griselda for her work at preserving the knowledge others would have ignored for vain and foolish reasons."

"Of course! Yes. What are the names? I wish I could take notes."

Agnes hands me a sheet of paper and a pencil, "Here. Write it down and it will be on your nightstand when you wake up."

Kate continues on, "The family names are Baylor, Brooks, Ward, Hale, Silseth, Rivas, Branch, Weaver, Rosales, Navarro, Villarreal, Yu, and Figueroa. Contact and meet with each family. Remind them of their duties. They signed the pact. There is no backing out and the consequences for refusal to uphold the contract are severe. Each family has a copy of the contract. Your copy is within the book itself."

I set aside the paper and pencil, all the names written down very carefully. "I will get on that. Now, I have a few more questions in addition to those I came here with. First, am I visiting you in a place in a certain time or are you shadows of the selves you were, left as a spell to guide? In my time most of the lore has been forgotten. I am working to make it more available, but in the meantime, there is so much I don't know. Is there an index to the book? How do I find the contract? I feel like I should at least be acquainted with it before I wave it in people's faces."

Mary looks up from her knitting, "Oh my. The next generations have put themselves in the dark, haven't they? We are real, same as you. None of us are in our proper time when we are in this room. Each of us is pulled from a moment when we can be in ourselves. So while I may be napping, Kaliope there could be spinning and Agnes could be washing dishes. Or staring off into space when she should be writing letters. The room is the spelled part. We can choose not to attend right then, but mostly we all find it a rest and a joy. We do peek in on you from time to time, you are going to do great things. The book does not have an index. However, if you focus on what you are looking for with your hands flat on the closed book, when you open it the pages will turn themselves to exactly what you are looking for, do try to be specific. Otherwise it wants to flip back and forth between pages for a time. If it does that, just slip a bookmark into each page and look at them at your leisure once it has calmed down again."

"Oh, well, that is going to be very handy. What do you know about vampires?"

Kaliope, ebony beauty of the group looks at me with curious eyes, "I might know a few things." She smiles and reminds me of a cat full of stolen cream. I bet she has got some knowledge. Well, here goes, "You all met Devon, right?" Each nods, "As it turns out, the guy that has been killing me and keeping me from my job is also his sire," gasps all around, "and he neglected his duties as Devon sire because he only sired him in order to enact his revenge on him."

Kaliope says, "That is an awful, dirty thing to do to someone. How he must have struggled over it all this time. They don't like to share information, vampires, but I don't know any that would have let this pass without challenging his maker over such gross neglect of his duties toward his fledgling. No matter the reason for the fledgling."

"I thought that might be the case. He tells me that he can't be caught seeking information because he will lose status in the vampire world. Is that true?"

Kaliope shakes her head, "No. They would educate him as he should have been educated by his sire, no matter what vampire he went to and word would spread about the sire and he may well be eliminated."

My eyebrows fly up, "Really? And that wouldn't kill Devon when his sire died?"

Kaliope scrunches her face at me, "What? No. That isn't how it works. Oh Sweet Lady, does he think he will die if his sire does? Is that why he hasn't turned you yet?"

"Yes. That is exactly why. Charles, his sire, has kept killing me in each reincarnation. Except this one. In part because Devon stayed away from me this time. And also because this time he has decided he would like a different kind of torment for Devon… He wants me to love him." I look away from the shock on their faces. This is so embarrassing.

Kaliope says, "Child, this is no shame of yours. He is the awful, debased creature looking to hurt everyone he comes in contact with. You hold your head up and don't let his foulness shame you. Why does he hate Devon so much?"

"Devon says that Charles holds him responsible for the death of his mother. They were at a market when someone ran up and stabbed Charles' mother. She died there in the dirt while Devon was running for the doctor. He said that Charles blamed him immediately, so it must be that he didn't get the doctor there in time."

Agnes nods, "Perhaps. Or perhaps it has nothing to do with him. We aren't likely to know without spell casting to see it. I don't think Devon is a liar, but he may not be aware of the reason."

Kaliope looks back to me, "Tell your man to talk to some-one. There are a great many things he needs to know and you should be turned as soon as possible. You need to be able to fend Charles off. The speed is the problem. Being an air affinity witch you have the ability to deal with him, but if he gets to you before you can call the winds… Well. Nothing good will come of that."

I nod, "That's how I feel too."

"Tell your Devon to talk to a vampire. Oh dear, you are starting to wake up! Remember our discussion from tonight and don't forget to contact those families! The names will be on the table next to your bed!"

I shake my head yes to them; I feel very strange as I see my body fade away to nothing and my eyes open to sunshine and Devon standing next to the bed holding a cup of coffee for me. I sit up and look over at the bedside table as I take the coffee from him. There is the list, just like Agnes promised. I have got to look up that contract today and start seeking out these families. Wait, didn't Devon say he kept in touch with them? "Darling, are you still in contact with the families?"

"Yes, of course. Why?"

"Because the witches told me I need to get in contact with the families and remind them of the contract. We talked about you too, and you are in for a surprise, my love. One, you won't die if Charles does. Two, what he did was a punishable offense. You need to tell Billy. He will train you in all the things you should have been taught by your sire to begin with, but were not taught. It was his duty, and he dropped the ball."

14

Twenty minutes later we are in his office where I am sitting and watching him go through a whole filing cabinet… "So why don't you have the contact info stored electronically?"

He never even looks up as he says, "Because this gives me a feeling of stability and permanence through time that electronic files don't."

I turn that over in my mind as I watch him check files and put them back, grumbling to himself the entire time. "Well, I guess. I would have had an argument if you said it was for the convenience of having everything organized right there in front of you."

He lifts his head to level a narrow-eyed gaze at me before going back to his search and I ask him, "Why don't you have this alphabetized or labeled or something?"

He sighs into his files, "Not going to let this go, are you?"

I shrug, "Nah."

"I kind of liked it being unorganized when I started it. It was an accordion folder, and it seemed a little rakish. It was my thing. Then it was a file box. Now it is two giant, four-drawer cabinets, and it got well out-of-control years ago. I don't keep things for my accountant in here because I would spend so much time every year just trying to find anything. I haven't actually been in these cabinets for a few years. The idea of trying to create some order out of this chaos is daunting. So that is where I am at with it. Satisfied?"

"Yes and no. I mean, you could hire someone to organize all that for you. They would need input from you but, that could become a much more functional part of your life if you like it."

He stops and looks over at me perched on his desk with my second cup of coffee, "I guess I could… It really never occurred to me that I could do that."

"You certainly could. I mean, we could even hire a vampire for the job if you wanted. Or a human in the know. Honestly, it looks like you need a whole personal assistant. If it didn't offend you, there are a lot of shifters that could make great personal assistants. I know lots of them end up with all this training that they don't get to use to the fullest extent because they have problems keeping work and shifter life separate. It works the same way for a lot of witches. Do vampires have those problems?"

From the depths of the files I hear "Only the young ones without the monetary resources that come from having lived for a very long time."

"That makes sense. I—"

"Found it!" Devon snatches a folder out of the drawer, the picture of a triumphant knight as he holds it up in the air briefly. He is adorable. Flipping through the file he walks over to me, "Here they are, all thirteen family contacts in one file. What family will you start with contacting?"

He hands the file over and I set it on my crossed ankles, opening it to see what information he has kept on these witches. He has them sorted by family and though the blood members of the family are all listed, the majority of the information is used on the contact person, and includes his impression of them along with their behavior when they met. Well, that could be really handy.

I remember that he asked a question, "Oh, um, I don't know which one I will start with? I mean, I thought I would go alphabetically but with the information you have included, well, I may tackle the one that was most rude first. I may have to do a bit of travel to get this done properly."

He nods, "I spent a year every decade or so visiting the families and sightseeing, maybe we could do that together this time?"

I grin at him, "I would love that! We are going to have to break it up into smaller bites, I have the foundation to see to as well. Until it is fully set up, I am going to be very hands on. After that, I will probably choose a board of people to take care of the day-to-day runnings of the foundations' many projects."

He leans on his desk and slips an arm around me, "I think this is going to be the best year I have had in a very long time." I lean into him, the scent of patchouli and books wrapping around me. I breathe deeply, I love the way he smells. "I think you may be right Devon, this is going to be the best year ever in a very long time."

15

Wandering off to my office with the file and the sheet of paper with all the names tucked into the file, I meet Natasha on her way into the office. It started out as mine, but really at this point it is our office. She spends at least as much time as I do in there. I think today is the day we fix the spell. "Natasha, here is what I am thinking we work on today." I juggle my coffee over to the hand with the file in it so I can take her hand and we can both go through the barrier, "First, this whole barrier thing. Let's fix it. I want you to be able to move freely in and out of here, this is your office just as much as it is mine anymore. Besides, if something happens to me, what if you are in here? Or Devon? Or anyone else? You could be trapped until you figure out how to undo the spell." She nods as she starts pulling items out of the cabinet. "After that, I talked to the witches last night, and they told me about another facet of this whole deal that Devon probably wasn't even aware of, but that Griselda would be really happy to hear." She stops and turns to face me, eyebrows raised, "Oh really? And what is that?"

"The witches said that those families signed a contract to preserve the lore and spells of their families **and** the families in their region, any that they could get in touch with. The contract apparently specifies some consequences for them if they refuse to hold up their end of the bargain. They send their thanks to Griselda too, for all her work to preserve the lore of the families she came in contact with. They say she has done us all a great service. Now, I wonder, these families. Did they continue to collect the lore and pass it off as their own, or did they simply fall out of the practice of collecting it? Or choose not to?"

"Grams is going to feel so honored that these past witches sent that message to her. We need to go over there and tell her in person."

"Definitely. It's been a minute since we saw her. Oh, and the witches also told me how to find stuff in the book! The contract is in there and I was like, well I need to give that a read before I go trying to remind them of it. Maybe have a leg to stand on or something, ha. So, basically we have the book closed and," I step over to the lectern that holds the book and set the file and my coffee down on the table next to it. Closing the book, I place my hands on it, "then you put your hands on it, focus on what you are seeking, and open the book." I focus on the contract the thirteen families signed and open the book. The pages flip forward from the point at which I opened it, coming to rest on a page near three quarters of the way through the book. Natasha comes to stand next to me and we look in amazement at the contract. "This is the coolest thing ever." I say as I skim the contract. Natasha nods, "It really is. Don't suppose they told you how to combine entries?"

"Shit. I forgot to ask. I will go back to see them soon. This is crazy... Apparently if they refuse to fulfill the contract, their family loses the ability to practice magic until they have made amends to the magical community. Ugh, it says I would be the one to say when they had made amends enough to reinstate their magic. If I am reading this right, I will be able to reinstate their magic by doing a blessing ceremony. I don't have to do anything for them to lose their magic. If they are not abiding by the terms set forth in the contract, their powers will slowly weaken over generations until they aren't magical anymore, but once I show up and press the issue, if they don't comply they lose their magic immediately. Wow. They were really serious about chronicling our history."

Natasha nods, still reading the contract. "It mentions here toward the end that they can be released from the contract by you for one of two specific reasons. That also requires a ceremony but the reasons are the family dying out or if it isn't safe to be collecting lore because of witch hunts."

"Hmm, well, that is pretty reasonable. And it gives those in need a way out." I pick up the folder and open it, "So all these families could be losing their magic over this." I flip through the pages of contact info to find the closest possible family. "Oh wow, there is a family living here in North Carolina." I tug their info out of the stack and begin to read the file, "So these are the Hales, they live over in Pinetown? Where even is that? Would you look that up for me, please?" Natasha grabs her Mac and taps away at the keyboard. The rest of the file lists the family. "Ok, so this family includes Rebekah, Natalya, Arlene, Katrina, and Marla. That seems like only one set of kids. Or maybe that is a couple generations… Why doesn't he say in here? They all live at the same place, I guess, so that should make it easier—"

"Found it. Ok, that place is over near the coast. It looks like a little town, not much to it. But also not super far away. You could get there in around 3 hours driving. Which means this one could be a day trip."

"Oh, perfect. Maybe we could go and make a stop at the beach if it is a nice day. Maybe get a room or five off the beach, wait… a cabin or something would be better. That would probably be safer too. Make a note that we need to get this on the schedule. So we don't forget. Now, I wonder what vampire information might be hidden in here?" I close the book and put my hands on the cover, focusing on the word vampire. Opening the book and it is flipping from page to page. It settles on a page for a few seconds, then flips to the next. I watch it go through the sequence once, making note of page numbers. The second go round I start to place little strips of paper to mark the page and it keeps going until I have marked each of the pages.

I read it out loud so we aren't both crowding the lectern, "The first page describes vampire physica. They have two phases, living and dead. The live vampires still breathe, blood still runs through their veins, and they can still enjoy food. Though they do not need nearly as much. The live form can continue living indefinitely. They usually move into the second phase through accident or murder. In this dead phase they don't breathe, can't eat or drink most things. Spirits are able to be consumed… Spirits? OH! Alcohol! They never get tired or winded."

Natasha nods, "Even dead vampires need a stiff drink occasionally."

Chuckling, I move on to the next page, "This one is titled 'How to Kill a Vampire.' You can only kill them one at a time, killing one does not kill those that were turned by that vampire. Good to know. Beyond that, they say that you just have to be a lot more thorough than if you were killing a human. Staking them through the heart is just going to piss them off. They will heal from most things, the difference is time. It says that 'unwary vampires have woken in the grave, having to dig themselves out and lent credence to the idea that vampires sleep in graves and coffins and that is where one should hunt them'. Oh my gosh, can you imagine? Waking up and having to dig your way out of a whole grave?" We both shudder at the idea. I flip over to the next marked page and begin to read, "Oooo, this one says vampires do not age in any physical manner. But their minds do, and that is why they avoid the younglings. I wonder what they mean by younglings? And vampires are not exempt from reincarnation. Oh, that is good to know. I need to tell Devon, it will relieve him to know this. Ok, last page. *The Vampire Code*. Sounds very official. According to this, if you turn them you are responsible for training them. If you don't train them, they can hold you responsible for their actions during their first twenty years as a vampire. The consequences range from imprisonment to death. If you turn a child, that is a death sentence for you. It doesn't say it is a death sentence for the child… I need to ask Billy about that. What happens to a turned child? Stay out of the public eye, that makes sense… Don't be a serial killer. I think that could have gone under stay out of the public eye. Be discreet if you must kill humans, better not to kill them—"

"It really says that? The part about better not to kill them?"

"Really, really. Heal bite marks with your saliva. Leave no witnesses, a.k.a. snitches go in ditches. Stay away from religion, you'll start a whole hunt."

"Yaaasss! That one."

"First twenty years you may turn no one because you are the vampire equivalent of a small and impulsive child. It doesn't say that last bit, but I figure that is the reason."

Natasha laughs, "It sounds about right though. I can imagine a lot of people actin' a fool for a while after they get turned. People act the fool from about eighteen to twenty-five without becoming vampires. It must get worse with the addition of that."

"Hmm, yeah. I'm sure. Can you just see some 21-year-old white boy wandering around with vampire strength and abilities looking to start trouble? No one would be safe." My phone starts ringing and I realize we still haven't fixed the barrier when I look up and see Devon on the other side. "Ugh, ok. Soon as he leaves, we fix the barrier." I walk over and touch his hand so he can come through. Devon wraps me up in his arms as he walks through the barrier. I soak up all the warm fuzzies this has me feeling. He releases me while still keeping an arm around me. I walk him over toward the lectern and show him *The Vampire Code*. We watch his face as he reads all it contains, by the end he is a little pale. "Charles would be dead if anyone knew the truth about him turning me. I wonder if he even knows this? He turned me not long after he was turned and he definitely did not train me. This was in here the whole time? How did you find it?"

"I told you that I dream-walked to talk to the witches from the past. The filled me in on a lot of things, like how to find things in the book. So what did you come to talk about? I think this was not it."

"Oh! Yes. Well, I thought, maybe we could do it this weekend. If you were ok with that?"

"Oh love, we can go do it right now if you want," I hear Natasha snickering, "you don't have to set an appointment for that."

Devon grabs my butt with both hands and pulls me over to press against the front of him and he growls into my ear, "If that was what I had come here for we would have left already." A shiver runs through my body and I think I would like to leave with him now, then he nips the spot where my neck and shoulder meet. I moan and press into him, he pushes me back. I look up at him, disappointed that he stopped. I see his fangs have extended a little and his eyes have managed to get even darker. He looks like he is holding himself back from eating me up. Oh Sweet Lady, I don't think I want him to hold back. If it feels that nice, put me on the menu, baby! He closes his eyes, still holding me at arm's length, and I watch his fangs retract. His eyes open again and they are back to their usual dark pools. He clears his throat, "I, um, ahem, I was thinking that we, that I could turn you this weekend, if that works for you? I need to pick up some more blood because you will need it at first, but after that, well, I thought this weekend would just be a good time to do it, I mean that. Get you turned. Into a vampire."

I am a little shocked. I look at Natasha, and she is grinning and shaking her head yes. I meet his eyes and he looks so concerned, like he thinks I am going to back out now. "I would love that. Um, just to clarify though, will there be sex involved when we turn me? Because I think it would be a missed opportunity if we skipped that."

This warm, throaty chuckle bubbles up out of him as he says, "I think we can do that. And now, I am going back to my office. It is suddenly very warm in here." I cup his face in my hands and give him a quick kiss, as he turns to go I give his butt a smack too. I don't even see him spin around and grab me, crushing me to his body, and kissing me along the line of my neck before planting a toe curling kiss on my lips. He sets me back down and holds me up till I am balancing myself, he takes my hand and holds it as he strolls through the barrier. I realize that during all that he actually moved me over next to the barrier and I never noticed.

Natasha says, "Girl, you two are making it hot in here! I need to find myself a lover for a night or three. Maybe I can get Shawn to make a house call? Think it would offend anyone if I bring another vampire over?"

"I don't know? We should check with Devon, but first we fix the barrier."

16

I wake up Tuesday morning to my phone ringing. It's Maggie calling to tell me that everything is ready for the sale to go through, we just need to meet at Ben's office to sign the papers. We agree on Friday; it seems like a great way to start the weekend. I slip off to the bathroom and take care of morning business quickly before running back to the bed. Devon is still laying in the bed, warm and naked. I cozy up to him and ask, "Wanna celebrate my new building before we go downstairs?"

"I thought you'd never ask."

AN HOUR AND A SHOWER LATER, WE MAKE IT DOWNSTAIRS. Devon works on making coffee while I sit at the island.

Billy wanders in and sits to wait for the coffee as well. Long minutes later we all have coffee.

Billy sets his cup down and says, "I have news." Devon and I both look over at him, brows raised and cups still cradled. He takes another sip of his coffee and says, "I got in touch with the twins. They are working their way here. They also said they would go see if Malachi would come too, and that it would take them longer to get here because of where they have to go to find him."

Devon says, "That is great. Where is he that is so hard to get to that it will take them longer?"

Billy shrugs, "I dunno. Doesn't matter to me, so I didn't ask. Oh, they also said quit changing your damn number."

"Uh, yeah. I am on it. No number changing so people can get in touch with me. Sorry about that."

I chime in to take the focus off Devon, who is clearly not enjoying this line of conversation. "I got a call from Maggie this morning. Everything is going through and the building is officially mine as of Friday when I go sign papers for miles. And Devon is going to turn me this weekend so that will be another worry off the list." Billy looks at Devon, brows raised and mouth open. I continue on, "So what do you know about *The Vampire Code*?" Now Billy's slack jaw is focused on me again, and I reach over to gently push his chin up. That seems to snap him out of his shock and he asks, "How did you convince him?

How did you hear about the code? You aren't supposed to know about that until you are turned. Did you tell her early?"

Devon shakes his head no, "Actually, I didn't know about the code myself until she showed me the copy in the Chronicle. It would seem my sire has a lot to answer for in regards to the code."

Billy is pale by the time Devon finishes. He takes a sip of his coffee, opens his mouth to speak, closes it, takes another sip. He repeats the process a few times before he is finally able to speak. "You, Devon, you mean to tell me that you didn't know about the code at all? Were you not trained? Did no one guide you through your first two decades?" Devon nods his head to answer each question and Billy continues, "This could be really bad. I have to ask, what did you spend your first two decades doing?"

"I didn't do a whole lot, really. Spent a lot of time drinking from criminals. It took me a while to reconcile the blood drinking. I really thought I was damned forever. I met Fate for the first time before I was twenty years into being a vampire. I really didn't want to be caught, and I didn't know any vampires beyond Charles. But he didn't stick around to train me. From what I understand, he was still new himself. I think his father turned him, but I can't be certain. He was pretty crazed the night he showed up and turned me.

When I woke up the next morning, I was a vampire and alone. I remembered bits and pieces of the night before. I left the little town I lived in. There was blood all over the house I lived in and it was trashed from the fight. I dug up a body from the local graveyard and put it in the house and torched the place on my way out. I didn't want any of the people I knew to find out what had happened to me. It was a lot easier to walk into a different life back then than it is now."

Devon runs a hand through his hair, sending it in all directions. I reach over and give him a one-armed hug for comfort. He wraps an arm around me and goes on with his story, "I wandered around for a while. I met Fate probably somewhere in the second decade? I had pretty well adjusted to my life then, and I was a lot better by then. Still feasting on criminals, but they were as plentiful then as they are now. It was no problem to hide the bodies then either. I figured out the saliva trick pretty early on so I was never outed that way, or any other way for that matter. I was very cautious by nature.

Plus, I was always trying to hide from Charles. He followed me like a hound on the scent. When I saw Fate for the first time, I was done. I could no more leave her than I could kill myself. I fell that hard, that quick. I settled in the area and set to courting her. It took no time at all. She didn't have parents then either. She did have some women, witches, that had found her as a babe and took her in. Weird how that happens to you a lot. We should probably look into that at some point. After I found her I was focused on her. Charles had guaranteed I wouldn't kill him by telling me that I would die too." Billy opens his mouth to contradict that statement and Devon holds his hand up, "I know, I know. That isn't true. Yes, that is why I was so reluctant to turn Fate. I didn't want to save her by killing Charles only for the both of us to die."

Billy's face would be comical were the conversation not so serious. He recovers his composure and says, "That is why you have avoided killing him all this time?"

Devon looks away, "I thought I would die and be out. Out of the reincarnation cycle. Out of life. Out of Fate's life. I thought that if he died, I would never see her again." His throat works as he tries to hold himself together. I lean into him and give him a squeeze with the arm still around his waist. He gives me a light squeeze back, clears his throat and looks back to Billy, "You understand a lot more now I am sure. You won't use it against me, will you?"

"What? No! How — Mate, you have a lot still left to learn. One of us is going to train you up. Your sire has a lot to answer for because of the way he neglected your educa-tion." Billy gets up and begins to pace back and forth, "You do not understand the things you could do, you can't. No one has told you. Or shown you. You have been walking around an uneducated vampire, a newb for two hundred plus years. Oh, that is so not good." He stops mid rant and looks to Devon, "Have you turned anyone? Ever?"

"No. The only one I ever thought about turning was Fate and Charles has killed her before I could every time."

"Oh, that is great news!"

I snarl at Billy, "What part of Charles killing me repeatedly is great news?"

He stops again, "Not that part. The part where he hasn't actually turned anyone. I mean, if he had turned you that would have been fine because the two of you would have stayed together, anyway. But, if he had turned someone and not trained them… Well, he would have been in just as much trouble as Charles. We don't have a counsel, but we do have a hierarchy. It is the eldest vampires that set the code in place, and they are the ones that enforce it. Any of the elders can and will enforce the code on the spot. And guys, Malachi is an elder. We aren't even really sure how old he is, to be honest. The twins think he is around six hundred years old, but they are just guessing from the fact that they heard rumors about Malachi when they were children that placed him in the area about two hundred years before that. I do know for sure that he is one of the elders and there aren't a bunch of them. Well, we don't think there are a bunch of them. For all we know there could be and they are hiding for the quiet."

I feel the color must have drained out of my face. "He wouldn't be upset about Devon turning me now, right?"

"What? Oh, no. Devon has been around for well over his two decades and has proven that he isn't going to cause problems even without knowledge of the code. Someone would have heard about it well before now. Admittedly, there have been whispers about Charles before now. We never had one of the vampires he sired tell their story. Mostly because they all died long before anyone else got to them. He kept the others with him to train, everyone except you. Of course he also killed the others, so maybe you dodged a bullet there. He has been questioned about why his apprentices die so often, and he always says that he is just a poor judge of character."

Devon scrunches his brows, "I think I know what happened to some of his apprentices. Definitely the most recent one. He was sent to mug Fate, and it was actually because of him that she got access to all her memories in one fell swoop. I killed him in her defense. A few of his other apprentices went out in a similar manner."

"Oh. Well, that is fine. No one will look twice at that. They came to you, correct?"

"Yes."

"Then you were defending, no issue for you. However, Charles sending his apprentices against you repeatedly will reflect poorly on him when the elder looks at his history to see if there are any redeeming qualities that could give cause to spare his life."

Natasha comes stumbling into the kitchen just then and Billy steps over to help her to a stool before getting her a cup of coffee fixed just how she likes it. I exchange a look with Devon that leaves us both grinning. Natasha notices and asks, "What are you grinning for?"

My grin gets wider as I answer her, "Billy sure is being really nice to you this morning. Anything we should know about?"

She scowls at me, "No. Absolutely not. He is just trying to prevent me setting his ass on fire for all the aggravating things he says all day. Or possibly trying to get me awake and capable of restraining myself before he starts in on me."

Billy grins as he places the coffee in front of her. "I'll never tell which one it is."

Natasha scowls at him as she picks up her coffee, "Whatever laughing boy. The day is young, I might set you on fire yet."

Devon gets a pained look on his face, "Could we not set anyone on fire?"

Natasha waves a hand in his direction, "I probably won't ever follow through on the threat. I haven't yet. On other topics, if I wanted to have a friend over, a male friend, would there be an issue with that?"

Billy freezes for a brief moment and then carries on like nothing happened. Interesting. Devon shrugs, "I don't see any problem with it."

She looks over the rim of her coffee cup, "Even if the friend is another vampire? Or shifter? Or witch?"

Devon shrugs again but I am watching Billy who is now drinking his coffee with a lot of care and focus. Devon says, "As long as you are quite sure they pose no threat, you live here too. You can have guests as you please."

Billy sets his cup in the sink and excuses himself. Devon throws a questioning look my way, but I wave him off. It should be fairly interesting to see how this plays out.

I tune back into the conversation, Natasha is relieved. She was concerned that it might be an issue and would have gone out to take care of her needs had it been a problem. I smile into my cup; I think she is about to have someone here looking to spend more time with her and being a lot more obvious about his intentions.

17

NATASHA

Billy has been acting weird ever since I asked about having male visitors over this morning. Alternating between gruff and sad. I do not have time for this nonsense. That is why I am stalking him now. He is hiding in some damn corner of this house and we are going to hash it out. I know he has the hots for me, and to be honest, I have been feeling something ever since that kiss we shared. The only place in this house that I haven't checked is his bedroom, so fine. Confront the lion in his own den. I stalk the hallway past Steve and John's rooms to stand in front of his door. I know he can hear me; I am pretty sure he can smell me. Assuming he is in there, that is. He could have left the house, but I don't think he did.

I knock on the door and wait. I hear him shift around in there, but he isn't coming to answer the door. So I bang on it like the police. Steve pops his head out of his room, sees me and grins, "Get him girl." He disappears back into his room as the door in front of me is snatched open. He looks mad. Good, I can work with fire. "What is your damn problem Billy?"

His jaw drops and snaps shut as I step closer to him, and he steps back. He snaps back, "I'm not the one pounding on people's door."

"No, you are the one hiding in his room like a small child afraid to face me." I take another step into his space and he backs up again. I keep advancing until he is pinned between me and the bed before I say, "You are obviously upset about the possibility of me having male callers over, so why not say something? Why not say something at any point after we shared the kiss? Hmm? Cat got your tongue?"

He mumbles, "I didn't think you wanted to get tangled up with a vampire…"

"Of all the dumbassed things…" I wave a hand at the door to close it and take the last step to close the space between us, winding my arms around his neck and bringing his face down to mine I whisper, "I like to be nibbled." Then I bring my lips to his and wait to see if he responds at all. There is no wait as he wraps both arms around me and kisses me with a ferocity I hadn't expected but am thrilled to find in him. He breaks the kiss, leaving us both breathless as he kisses and nibbles his way across my jawline and down my neck. My whole body shivers with need. I feel him laying us back on the bed and I open my eyes, prepared to do my part in getting us positioned properly on the bed when I notice we are floating over the mattress. "You can float? Really?"

He smiles, "Yeah. Most of us can, we just don't always share that." He flips us over so he is over me and gently sets us down on the bed, "Natasha, before we go any farther you need to know my conditions."

"Well, spit them out. If I can't deal, then I am going to need to go find some relief after this buildup."

"I am all in. If you are going to be with me, then it is all me. I don't share. If it doesn't work out, I will do everything possible to remain friends with you and to not get in the way of anyone else you choose to see. But if we go any farther, my condition is that I be your only until you say otherwise and then we are done with this kind of relationship."

I pretend to mull this over; I don't have to think about it really. Since the first night I saw him my fires have been running on high and he is all I have wanted with every fiber of my being. After a suitable time spent letting him wait, I tell him, "I agree to your terms, sir. I find them acceptable and here are mine — you need to take care of this fire you started right now."

He smiles slowly and says, "Terms accepted, let's see about quenching that fire."

❈ 18 ❈

FATE

The week is flying by, the day after tomorrow we go to sign the papers for the purchase of the building. I have a really awful feeling though, like something is going to go bad. I need to talk to Steve. I'll tell him and he will tell me I just nervous. That's all it is, nerves. I track Steve down to the living area, he is watching tv. "Hey, can I talk to you for a minute?"

He grabs the remote off the table and shuts the tv off as he says, "Sure, what's on your mind?"

I walk in and sit on the other end of the couch, "In a couple days we go and sign all the papers for me to buy the building. I plan on taking you and Owen. I just have a really bad feeling about it and I don't know why. I thought I should share that since you all are there to protect me."

He is silent, brow scrunched and deep in thought. I wait patiently for him to finish the thought, Goddess knows I appreciate when people do that for me. He finally looks me in the eye and says, "Fate, I think we should take this seriously."

My eyes go wide, "Really? Shit. I was hoping you would say I was just nervous about buying the building."

"Thing is, you aren't prone to being real nervous over things. Like I tell the young ones, the beauty of getting older is that you have been through some things and you get a little more difficult to rattle. I know you are a witch. Maybe just knowing things isn't your specialty but maybe there is something in the air and your ability is trying to warn you."

"Damn it. I was hoping for being an irrational female."

Steve chuckles, "Uh, sorry I can't help you there. What I can do is suggest we take at least one more person. My preference would be Ajah, she is a one I would want watching my back."

I nod, "I think you are right. I'll let you take care of that. I wish Charles would just go die already. Maude, too. Both of them are a pain in my ass."

Steve looks hard at me and seems to come to a decision, "You know, not that I want to talk myself out of a job but, if we went after them instead of waiting for them to come to us… Well, it would certainly take care of a problem for you."

Shrugging, I say, "You're not wrong, but I don't think I am ready to make those decisions. I feel like it should be defense. I think you are right and that would be the better way to handle it. I just am dealing with a lot right now. My parents glamouring me to be white, how they hated and feared me, I was adopted, my sister is a whole lunatic and had to be bound, not to mention all the people that want me dead… It's a lot. I can't add sending you all out to kill my enemies to the list of things I am carrying right now."

Steve nods, "I understand. I felt like I should put it out there, because none of these people are operating by the kinds of rules you are playing by and we may need to step up our game at some point."

"We'll burn that bridge when we get to it. For now, I need to get to work. I'm sure Natasha is already up there working. Thanks Steve, I appreciate your help and your honesty."

"Anytime Fate, anytime."

I WALK INTO THE OFFICE AND THERE IS NATASHA WORKING away, hair up and love bites on her neck. Fascinating. "So Natasha," I wait for her to turn and look at my grin, "how'd you get those love bites?"

Natasha actually blushes and says, "I might have hunted Billy down and made a deal with the devil..."

I grab a chair and sit, ready to hear all the details. She sighs, "We aren't getting any work done until I tell you are we?" I shake my head no with a big grin. She sighs again and starts talking, "He was alternating between sad and angry after he heard me talking about having someone over. But he never came and talked to me about the kiss like he said he would, so I thought he had changed his mind. I went hunting him and found him in his bedroom. After a little cat-and-mouse game, he told me that if we went any further, he wanted to be my only one because he wouldn't share. He also said that if I changed my mind about being with him, then I could walk away, no problem. By that time I was pretty fired up and so was he. I agreed to his terms, and we had some of the best sex I have ever had in my entire life."

I squeal with joy, "Oooo girl! I am so happy for you! You two have been circling each other since you met. Devon and I were beginning to wonder if you and him would ever just go ahead and admit the way you felt about each other."

"Yeah, I was a lot worried that I would catch feelings for him. It was a valid concern. I have definitely caught feelings for him. Admittedly, the feelings were happening way before the sex, but pot-ay-to, pot-ah-to. Besides, dating a vampire while I am thinking I want to be turned is no bad thing."

"Aw, I love it. I hope you are both really happy together. Now, in a complete topic change, I need your help with some things."

Natasha raises her brows at me, "Well that is what you hired me for and I am your friend so... what do you need?"

"I have a really bad feeling about Friday. I don't know why and I couldn't even say what part of tomorrow it is about. So I want to set things up in a way that you could keep on doing things and keep the foundation moving forward, even if I am not able to take part."

"Whoa there. What? Have you talked to anyone about this? Besides me?"

"I talked to Steve first. I was hoping that he would say I was being silly. He didn't. Instead, he suggested that I am getting a warning of sorts from the air. He also suggested we bring Ajah tomorrow. I agreed. But, if I go to the hospital or die or something, I want things to keep moving forward. That way when I come back, things will be in place for me. And I hope you will still become a vampire and be here to find me. Maybe this will all come to nothing, but I want to be prepared."

She presses her lips together, "I don't like this. But I do see your point and why you would want to take precautions.

I'm in. And I will be here waiting if you die. Because I am going to kick your sorry ass for leaving me alone for so long. Even if I do have Billy. Male friends and lovers are never the same as a good girlfriend."

"Thank you. Thank you for understanding and for being a real friend. I don't know what I would do without you. Ok, I am going to have Benjamin draw up a power of attorney so you can sign for and do things in my name. I will also give him instructions to work with you if anything should happen to me so that all my… stuff can be taken care of. I need you to take on the Chronicler stuff until I can return. You don't have to go see the families, just work on the books. Keep collecting the books from your Grams. Will you do that?"

"Of course."

"Oh, thank Goddess. Ok. I was thinking that tomorrow we could head over to see the Hales. Feel up to a drive into the country?"

"I do. We are bringing bodyguards, right?"

"Of course. I was also hoping the drive would help clear this sense of impending doom I have hanging over my head."

"It could happen."

"Yeah. It could. Twelve lords a-leaping could fly out of my ass and yeet themselves out the window with all that leaping, but I don't think that is going to happen either. Let's get to work."

$\maltese$ 19 $\maltese$

It is hot outside. We all climbed in the Suburban to make the trip and for all of a minute we thought we would ride with the windows down. Then we remembered that we would be driving through swamp and the southeast. We put those windows up and cranked the ac. That was hours ago. We are almost there; the gps has us going down some crazy dirt road that looks more like a goat path. Oh wait, there's the house. This is their drive-way. Damn. That is a nice house for a driveway like that. Maybe they don't want visitors. Too bad. I throw air shields up over all of us and get out of the truck. Walking to the front door, it opens before we get to it and a woman with a gun steps out onto the porch. "Can I help you find the way out of here?"

"No. We know the way out. This is the Hale residence, right?"

She cocks the gun, "What of it?"

"I'm the Chronicler."

"Prove it."

"The only way I know to prove it is by taking away your magic for not upholding the contract, is that really how you want to do this?"

She lowers the gun. "No, it isn't. I guess you might as well come in."

I come to the door, and she turns to walk farther into the house. Steve grabs the door and holds it as the rest of us file in behind the woman. She leads us straight through the house and to a porch out back, setting the gun down by the door she introduces everyone, "I'm Rebekah. This is Natalya, Arlene, Katrina, and the baby is Marla."

"Nice to meet you all. I am Fate, this is Natasha, Steve, Ajah, and Owen."

"We don't get many people your color out here. Less of the ones like her," she jerks a thumb toward Ajah, "and the ones that do come out are usually looking for trouble."

"Interesting. I take it white suburbans with groups of well-dressed people of color wander the streets here just looking for trouble?" Rebekah glares at me for calling her out like that, but I don't give a damn. She's pissing me off already. "I didn't come here to discuss any of that. I came here in my role as Chronicler. Have you upheld the contract?"

"I don't see why you are here now. You been ignoring us all these years, we ain't seen no one since my Ma was young and it was just that feller that was filling in. Where have you been all this time?"

"Not that it matters, but I spent a lot of it dead. I am here now. And I know at this point your family's magic has been on the decline or you wouldn't have needed a gun to threaten me with at the door with all this water around. Now, this is the last time I will ask. Have you upheld the contract? Have you been collecting the lore of your community? The spells? Or have you been holed up here hiding from everyone?"

Natalya says, "Mama, stop being hateful. If you can fix our magic, do it. Or I will." Rebekah glares at her and she glares right back as Arlene says, "Fine. I am going to get the books. You are being ridiculous, mama. Age is no excuse for your attitude." Arlene excuses herself, saying that she will be back shortly. Rebekah continues to glare at everyone, Natasha and I don't care. Steve, Owen, and Ajah simply plant their feet and cross their arms. Natalya asks us if we would like anything to drink, eyeing Rebekah, I tell her no, we're good. It just doesn't seem like the greatest pan to accept a beverage in the house of a water witch family when one of them is unhappy with you. Natasha says, "So how are you all related?"

Katrina answers, "Marla is my baby, Arlene is my mama and Natalya is her sister. Rebekah is their mama, my grandmama."

I tell her, "Your baby is adorable. Is her dad at work?"

Rebekah's glare intensifies and Katrina looks sad as she tells us, "No. He's dead. All the men die shortly after the birth of their only child. That's why Mama and Natalya have different daddies. I don't think I'll have any more children."

Natasha and I exchange a look, "That's an odd occurrence for a family. It sounds almost," I look directly into Rebekah's angry eyes, "like your family has been cursed. Or something."

I see the fear bloom in her eyes as she looks away, I don't think they were cursed and I would bet this particular 'curse' will die with Rebekah. Arlene comes back, pulling a cart piled with books behind her.

I know my eyes aren't the only ones that go round at the sight of the pile of books in the cart. I say to her, "You all have been keeping the contract! But I see three or four whole grimoires. Did that many entire families die out?"

Rebekah gets up and walks over to stand in front of me, "People sticking their noses into the wrong places have a way of disappearing around these parts." I stand slowly, calling air to me and look her right in the eyes as I say, "People with so many secrets shouldn't make threats they can't back up. Should we lay all your secrets bare for your family now?"

"I don't have anything secrets!" Rebekah yells at my face before storming out the screen door. I watch as Natalya and Arlene share a look between them. Sitting back down I tell them, "If your mama causes you any further grief, let me know. Her powers can be bound without affecting yours and I think you will find that you all are a lot more powerful than you ever were now that I have been here and verified that you are upholding the contract. However, if it is found that the families in your community have disappeared for reasons owing to this family, if it isn't stopped by this family, then I will invoke the punishment of ripping the magic from this family."

Arlene replies, "We understand. And we will be taking care of the family issues. Mama was the most powerful of us back when she was young. Her magic has waned over the years, we are in our prime and our magic has just come in since you arrived. She won't be causing anymore problems. For any of us." She lays a hand on Katrina's shoulder as she says this, and I am left to wonder just how domineering that woman has been.

"Well, thank you for your time and for all the lore and grimoires you have collected. We will see ourselves out and leave the cart in the yard near the front door." I pull a card from my pocket, "Here is my number, call me if you need help." Arlene takes the card and slips it into her bra. I nod and we stand. Natasha grabs the handle of the cart and follows Steve and me to the front door, Ajah and Owen bringing up the rear. It is the work of a couple minutes to get the books and papers loaded into the back of the suburban, Owen drops the cart off near the front door. Once we are all in Steve turns the truck around, heading us all away from the Hale homestead.

I turn to look at Natasha, Owen, and Ajah in the back; "Was that not the strangest woman? I think she has been killing all the men in that family! That poor baby! Those poor girls!"

Ajah says, "I think you are spot on. That old woman has been doing terrible things for entirely too long. I hope her daughters handle her and are better people than she was."

Natasha nods, "Me too. That old woman is definitely a whack job and needs to be taken down. A lot. I wanted to slap the white off her, but you did fantastic at keeping your calm. I was impressed."

"Thanks. I wanted to slap her till I couldn't lift my arm, but I didn't want the baby to see me do that to her great grandma. So I settled with saying things to frighten the crap out of her. I wonder how many secrets does she think the girls in there don't know that they have already figured out, or at least suspect? I think Arlene and Natalya figured things out and just weren't willing to stand up to their mother for themselves. But as sad as Katrina is over her baby's daddy, I don't think they are willing to let that slide."

Ajah says, "Yeah. I think they were already plotting something for the old woman and we just made it easier."

I turn back to face front and ponder what Ajah said.

It is late when we get home, Devon and Billy are waiting in the kitchen when we arrive. Steve, Owen, and Ajah say hi and goodnight as they head straight for their rooms. I walk into the kitchen and hug my Devon. He asks, "Are you all hungry? Do you want me to make you a little something?"

I nod and ask Natasha, "How about you? Want anything?"

"Goddess yes! Chips and a soda don't cut it for me and I am not eating fast food."

Devon kisses my forehead and walks over to the fridge. Billy asks us, "So how did the mission go? Were they doing what they should or did you have to smack them down?"

I look over at Natasha; she shrugs with the shoulder not leaning on Billy. So I tell the story about how the trip went. Billy is amazed, "Holy shit Fate. That woman sounds like a murdering racist hiding out there in the swamps and abusing her family. I thought those type people were fairytales, stereotypes that didn't really exist."

"Oh, this lady definitely exists, and she fits all the stereotypes in so many crazy ways."

Devon walks over with two plates and sets one in front of me and the other in front of Natasha, "Maria actually made these up for everyone, in case they were hungry when they got home. She said she has some family out that way and it is a trip. It worried her that you all would only have fast food all day."

Natasha and I are too busy enjoying the baked chicken, broccoli with cheese, and mashed potatoes to answer right away. About halfway through the plate of food I am able to answer, "She was right, and she is amazing for leaving us plates. You are amazing for heating them up. Both of you are so very appreciated. So Maria has family in the area? I think I want to talk to her family. I wonder if they know the Hales or if they know of them? I definitely want to know more about that family. I think I want to investigate the other families a little before I show up. Did I mention she pulled a gun on us? I can't imagine what kind of tyrant she has been to her daughters and granddaughter all this time. She didn't look that old, but from the way her daughters spoke about her, she was really a lot older."

Natasha finishes her plate and chimes in with, "Yeah, I got the impression that Rebekah would be in the ground right now if it weren't for some shady dealings on her part. I don't know what she is doing, but she looked our age, early 40s. Her daughters looked in their 30s, though. The granddaughter was at least in her 20s. There is a lot to unpack with that family. They seem straight out of a V. C. Andrews book."

"Yes! That is the kind of vibe that family gives off!" Devon and Billy both look very confused. Natasha says, "Go ahead and finish eating, I'll educate them about the books. So V. C. Andrews wrote an entire series of books where the complete family was just evil except for one or two family members. Like things got seriously twisted in those books. There was one series where a brother and sister fell in love because they were locked away from everyone for so long when they were growing up. Another where it was a rags to riches kind of thing, but the rich family was just as horrible as her stepfather had been. That is the kind of vibe these people give off." Devon and Billy both look horrified and Billy says, "You both read these books? On purpose?"

I look away and say, "Yes. Sometimes when your life isn't so great reading about other people making it through their own really hard times helps. Those books helped a lot of confused teens understand that we don't have to follow in the footsteps our family has laid out for us. We can forge a different path and be better people." Devon rubs my back, "We're sorry. We didn't think before we spoke."

I lean into his hand a little, "It's okay. We all have our own ways of coping and learning. I don't think you all had the same conveniences we had when you were growing up and I am sure you both had your own issues to deal with in relation to your childhoods, you are just so old you have forgotten about them." Natasha bursts with laughter as Devon tickles me saying, "Old? Who are you calling old Miss?" Laughter spills out of me and I can hear Billy laughing as well. Devon stops tickling me and wraps his arms around me, drawing me close to him. He whispers in my ear, "Ready to go to bed?" I nod and we say our good nights to Billy and Natasha. Heading up the stairs we hear Billy ask her, "Your room or mine?"

They are adorable together, and I hope they work out. If not, I am sure it will only be awkward for the first twenty years or so…

As I strip my clothes off next to the bed, Devon says, "I got everything ready for tomorrow night."

I freeze for a minute. What is tomorrow night? OH! How could I forget? "Excellent. So tomorrow I will get my building signed and sealed as mine," a dark chill works its way up my spine and I just know I will not make it home tomorrow. So I will die on a Friday in this life. It seems so unfair that I can't even make it all the way through one life. "And tomorrow night I will be all vamped up. Unless you want to do it tonight? We could, I would be all right with that."

Devon shakes his head no, "I want to do this right for you. Rushing it will make it harder on you and make it not as nice an experience."

"Well, I don't mind. We could rush it a little. We would only be pushing it forward by one night."

"You already traveled over to the coast and back today, dealt with a racist white lady and her strange family; I think that is enough for anyone in one day. We'll do it tomorrow night, love," he comes around the bed to hold me, "and it will be a great first vampire memory. I need to make this the best possible experience for you. You aren't getting worried that you will back out tomorrow, are you?"

"No. I just felt like we could go ahead and do it tonight, I've been waiting for so long."

Devon tightens his arms around me and floats us onto the bed, "I learned a new trick today. And tomorrow will be worth the wait. Promise. Ok?"

I nod into his chest. The feeling that this will be my last night here for a very long time is deep in my bones now, "Make love to me Devon. I need to feel you one last time… as a human." I don't have anything concrete saying that I won't be back tomorrow and I don't want to scare Devon if it is just me being paranoid. He has dealt with too much loss in his life already. I am going to do everything I can to prevent him from losing me to death tomorrow. Maybe I can stay alive, if I am crafty enough. I forget all of it for a time as Devon takes me to a world where none of it exists.

Friday dawns and I stay in bed with Devon until I have to get ready to go to my meeting. When I finally get out of bed and go straight to the shower, I'll have coffee on my way out.

❧

SHOWER FINISHED, I GO OFF TO THE CLOSET TO PONDER what to wear to this. It is a momentous occasion for me, but I still feel like it is going to blow up in my face. That feeling of dread left for a few sweet hours last night while Devon and I made love, but it returned full force as soon as I wasn't distracted by him and the pleasure he gave me so easily. Going through the closet, it occurs to me that I am not a fighter, not in the conventional sense. If I get in a fight, it will be me using magic against someone, however they are trying to attack me. I settle on a black flowing skirt paired with a sapphire top. My closet looks a lot more like Natasha's now that our coloring is so similar. I wonder who my parents were? Why did they give me up? Is there a way for me to find out? Shaking my head, I finish dressing; I don't have time for this line of thinking. Looking at my shoes I decide on my trusty flats, they will be much easier to run in if I should need to move.

A few minutes later I am down the stairs with my hair up in a semi-messy bun and a little makeup applied. It is taking some time to figure out how to put makeup on a face I still don't know that well. I hate my adopted parents more than a little for betraying me this way. Forcing me to live a lie for their comfort. I am still amazed that it has taken very little time to see them as adoptive parents while adjusting to my unfamiliar face is messing me up still.

Maria has coffee ready and waiting for me, we chat for a little bit as I drink and wait for the others. She tells me that Devon and Billy left a short time ago after a call and Devon sends his love. I am a little relieved that he has gone somewhere, it will be easier to leave the house without leaving him in it. Natasha, Ajah, Steve, and Owen arrive in the kitchen and I hurry to finish my coffee so we can leave.

❧

FIFTEEN MINUTES LATER WE ARRIVE AT BENJAMIN'S office. We are all on high alert, but nothing seems even a little out of place. I breathe a sigh of relief and hope that this fear is all in my head. In the office we find Maggie, the building owner, their realtor, and Beth all in the reception area. Benjamin walks into the reception area shortly after greetings and introductions are finished. He invites us all to step into his office, where he briefly explains how things will work today. He will have the current owner and their realtor in the office with him first to sign all of their paperwork. Once they finish and leave, he will bring us in and we can sign all of our end of the paperwork and it will all be signed and sealed, ready to be delivered first thing Monday morning.

We go back to the reception area where Beth offers us beverages. I ask for coffee because oddly enough it calms my nerves when I am antsy. Probably has to do with the ritual of it. We sit out in the reception area for at least an hour while they go through their stack of papers to sign. My fears subside as we sit there so normally. I have been watching the traffic go by out the window and nothing out there has seemed even a little out of place. I am kind of relieved that my fears seem to have been all about the real estate transaction. Even Steve has relaxed a little. The door to Benjamin's office opens, and he escorts the owners and their realtor out of the building. Thankfully, the money was wired into Benjamin's account a few days ago, so he had the cashier's check here and waiting for today, making that one less thing I needed to concern myself with this afternoon. Coming back into the office, Ben says, "Ready to go sign for your new property?" As an enormous smile lights his face. Maggie and I stand as I tell him, "Yes! I can't wait! We are finally going to get my foundation going in a building outside of the house!" He laughs and follows us into his office.

We emerge an hour and a half later, tired but grinning. My hand had a little cramp in it briefly from all the signing, but it was quickly gone. Natasha gets up and walks over to hug me, "Congratulations! I am so happy for all of us! You are going to do so much good for the community with this building. I am really proud of you for having come so far since Charlie died. You are blooming girl, and it is the most beautiful thing to see." She hugs me tight and I hug her right back as I try to hold back the tears of joy from her words, not even my adopted parents ever told me they were proud of me. With one last squeeze I pull back telling her, "You're making my eyes leak, I don't want to fuck up my make-up." She laughs and dabs at the corners of her eyes too. I turn to see Ajah waiting for her hug with Steve and Owen in line behind her. My heart is so full to have all these people here and happy for me, congratulating me. I resign myself to messing up my makeup as I hug Ajah, Steve, and Owen, each in turn. Benjamin waits to congratulate me one more time at the door, telling me that he is proud of me too. I sniffle a little and Maggie tells him she will see him later for dinner as we walk out in the bright sunshine.

We stop at the sidewalk, and I hug Maggie, thanking her even as she is congratulating me. We say our goodbyes and she walks off to her car. Our group ambles over to the suburban, spreading out to each get into our spots. I open my door and hear Natasha scream. The feeling of dread crashes back on me as I drop everything and run around the truck to see what happened.

❧ 2 2 ❧

I get around the corner of the truck and my heart leaps into my throat. Steve is standing next to his open door with his hands out and open, Ajah and Owen are at the rear corner in the same stance. But my Natasha is being held in the air by her throat and the person holding her there is Charles. He sees me and gives Natasha a shake, turning back to face her and tell her, "One more time with the fire and I will pop your head off your body like a beer cap." He turns to me, "Fate, my darling. Come to me. Let's get out of here."

I know what I have to do. This is what I felt coming. "Put my friend down. If you want me to go anywhere with you she has to live. You are choking her." He lowers Natasha enough so she can support her weight on her toes and says to me, "Your move, Fate. I am being reasonable, for you. Think how much more reasonable I could be if you were with me. None of your friends would have to be hurt. Devon wouldn't have to die. My people have him right now. They will kill him if I don't call them soon and tell them to set him free."

"Why should I believe you, Charles? How do I know you will let everyone be free, alive, and unharmed if I go with you?"

"Ooh, clever girl to be so specific. Fine. I will swear an oath sealed with my blood. I, Charles Armstrong, swear that each of Fate Owens' friends here before me and those not in front of me along with her lover Devon shall go free, alive, and unharmed so long as Fate leaves with me." He bites the tip of a finger and drips a few drops of blood on the ground. I hit the blood with a binding magic. He can no more hurt them than he could stop the sun in the sky now. All it costs is me.

A fair trade for my family.

I nod to him, "Let me get my things." Everyone starts to protest and I hold up a hand, "Please don't make it harder." They fall silent as I gather my purse and phone from where I dropped them. Walking back around, I go to each of my bodyguards, hugging and thanking them. Ajah has tears running down her face as she whispers, "We will come find you, sister. Don't give up on us." I nod and turn, walking over to Charles. "Let Natasha down so I can tell her goodbye. Go stand over there. I will be right with you."

His eyes narrow, but he does as I say. I put an air cast around Natasha's poor neck, so bruised. I tell her that the cast will fade away by tomorrow. She hugs me, whispering, "Don't go with him." I whisper back to her, "We both knew I wouldn't make it home tonight. But I'll live this way and so will you and Devon." My voice catches on his name. I swallow and say, "Tell him I love him so much. I'll find a way back to you all. I promise." With one last squeeze, I release Natasha.

I turn and walk to Charles. He is smiling that awful smug smile that I want to slap off his face. I stop a couple steps from him and he grabs my arm, dragging me to his side. He levitates us away from my friends, my family. A few buildings away we land and he drags me over to a Porsche Cayenne. The car of a jackass, for sure. He walks me all the way around to the passenger door, opens it and says, "My Lady, your carriage awaits." Gritting my teeth I get into the car, I hate him so much.

He gets in the driver's side, pulls out his phone, calls someone and says, "Let them go." He listens for a moment, "Yes. Completely. Let them walk away unscathed. If any harm comes to them, I will end you." I can hear the voice on the other end say yes boss and then he hangs up the phone. My heart swells a little knowing that Devon and Billy will be safe, for now.

"Where are you taking me, Charles?"

He smiles big at me and cups my chin with his hand, squeezing just enough that I can't turn my face away from him, "Somewhere special. It's a surprise. I have a whole bunch of surprises planned for you tonight, my love."

"Don't call me that."

"Very well, do you prefer I call you my dearest?"

"Yes. That is fine."

23

Natasha

We make it home to find Devon and Billy just arriving home as well. They look how I feel. Guess Charles wasn't lying. The air cast is weird but handy. I can rub my neck, put my hand right through it, but my neck is completely supported and cushioned. I walk straight to Billy, tears spilling from my eyes as I whisper through my raw throat, "We lost her." He takes me in his arms as Devon howls in heartbreak and rage. Steve and Owen convince him to go inside, Billy and I follow him. I wait until he is done raging. The parlor is trashed by the time he is calmed. Billy, Ajah, and I wait in the kitchen for him. Steve and Owen waited outside the parlor for him to finish. It only took 45 minutes. So not terrible. We have been sipping the spiked teas Maria made for us after his crashing about woke her and her two helpers. She sent them back to bed, made us a pot of tea, and then she went back to bed herself. When he comes into the room, he still looks all fire and brimstone, but more in control. Steve and Owen trail in behind him. He asks, "So what exactly happened today?"

Ajah looks at me, and I nod for her to tell the story. She quickly tells him about the appointment and then gets to the part where Charles grabs me by the throat. It chokes her up, but she clears her throat and carries on with tears streaming down her face. She tells him about the promise Fate extracted from him before she would go anywhere with him and how Fate bound the promise with magic to ensure he could not renege.

After telling him about the hugs, she breaks downs and can't continue. Owen comes over to stand with her and comfort her as best he can while trying to hold himself together. I motion for Devon to come closer, I can barely whisper. He walks around the island and leans in closer to hear me say, "When she hugged me she said she knew she wouldn't make it home tonight, she'd had a feeling. She said this was better than she hoped. She was sure she would die today. She did this so we would all live. You, me, Billy, Ajah, Steve, and Owen. He told us that his people had you both. She said to tell you she loves you so much and that she will find a way back to us."

By the time that I finish, Devon has his arms around Billy and I, his head in my lap as he begins to sob.

FATE

Charles took me to a house across town. He has armed guards everywhere. He says that they are there because he is a drug lord and it is just so damn messy getting shot. I shrug. I don't care if they shoot up the whole damn house. He shows me a suite of rooms that he assures me are mine to do with as I please. He has his own suite down the hall. As we tour the suite he says is mine, he says, "You may do whatever you please in here with one exception. You may not have any man but me. You don't have to have me, but you will not have anyone else in place of me. Are we clear?" I raise an eyebrow at him, "Yes, your expectations are clear." He claps his hands together, "Good! You can leave your things here and we will go dine, unless, would you like to freshen up?"

"Yes, please."

"I will wait for you in the hall. Don't be too long!"

I roll my eyes as he leaves the room, shutting the door behind him. I walk over to the nearest drawer, open it and place an air shield specific to me in the drawer. I place my purse and phone inside the shield and closing the drawer I touch every drawer and flat surface in the room once. I stop to use the facilities and wash my hands in the bathroom, touching more surfaces on my way out. Anyone trying to figure out where I hid things will spend a minute looking, assuming that they are vampires, and try to sniff it out. Stepping out the door, I find him waiting in the hall with his back to the door, whistling. He turns as I close the door behind me, taking my arm he guides me back down the stairs to show me a lot more rooms I don't care about, until we get to his library. He walks me in saying, "I rarely come in here, but I like to collect books. So there is plenty of reading material for you during the time of your confinement."

"During the time of my confinement? How long do you intend to keep me here?"

"Until you realize we were meant to be Fate." He is completely serious as he utters those eight little words. Oh Sweet Lady, he plans to keep me forever. One of us is going to die, I just know it. I just shake my head. He walks over and taking my hand he lifts it to his lips and nips my knuckles before kissing them, "Come, dinner is being served. We should eat before we get to the big surprise tonight."

"The big surprise? Charles, what are you planning? You aren't going to do something awful to me, right? I mean, I know you have been the one killing me in my past lives, you aren't going to do that this time, are you?"

He laughs, "Oh Fate, I am sorry about that. I never got to know you before. I didn't realize that you were meant for more than just revenge against Devon. I should have swept you off your feet and away from him the first time he met you. I hope you will forgive me for our shared past eventually, I was wrong to kill you like that."

"Really? You were wrong? You think?" We reach the dining room and it has one of those ridiculously long tables in it with two places set at the far end. He guides me to the seat at the end of the table and takes the one to the right of me. His wait staff enters, serving us with steak and risotto and asparagus. It is all cooked very well and I sure his chef is amazing, but it tastes like sawdust to me. I ask Charles, "Why do you have such desire for revenge against Devon, anyway? What did he do to cause you to torment him for a couple centuries or so?"

Charles looks over from his food, "Do you really want to hear the tale?"

"Yes, I do." I say before forcing myself to take another bite.

He shrugs and says, "Well, if you insist. We grew up together. We were like brothers, and near inseparable. My father wasn't the greatest, but my mom was a saint. I don't know how she put up with him or us. We were in the market one day and my mother was acting strange. She had brought myself and Devon along with her, which was nothing unusual. Then she grabbed the both of us and tried to rush us off somewhere when someone stabbed her. Devon said he would go find help and ran away.

While he was gone my mother warned me that it was his fault and not to go home with him. She died just after she warned me away from him. She good as told me that it was Devon's fault she died. I have never forgiven him for killing my mother. Especially since he has never been willing to admit to his part in the deed. That is why when my father found me one night years later and turned me into a vampire I knew, he had just given me the gift that would allow me to avenge my mother's death."

"Your father turned you?"

"Yes. As I said, he was not the greatest father ever, but he did leave me with one last gift that has made all the difference."

"I see. So did he train you or?"

He barks a harsh laugh, "No. He showed up one night, turned me and was gone when I woke a vampire the next morning. I only knew what had happened because he had told me what he was going to do, said time was the only gift he could give me. So he gave me all the time in the world. I am grateful for it, his gift has allowed me to do and be so many things. I never saw him again after the night he showed up and turned me."

Hmm, I will just file that away. Charles continues on, telling me about his early life as we eat dessert. It looks lovely, but I can't taste any of it. Apparently Charles has been a criminal for his entire life. He started with petty crimes and expanded as he learned more. He had made enough money that he had put his criminal activities mostly on hold when the drug trade blew up. So he went to Columbia and took over one of the drug lord's operations, by walking in and ripping out his throat with his teeth, then drinking his fill as the blood gushed out over his face and body. He threw the body down and sat in the drug lord's chair. The guys that worked for the now dead drug lord just never questioned him after that.

He turned the ones that proved their loyalty and worth. His operation grew, and now his is one of the largest in the world. His Durham estate is just one of many. "Fate, now that we have dined, let us retire to the garden." I stand and he takes my elbow, guiding me out to the garden whether or not I want to go. We stroll along paths dimly lit with small lights on either side till we come to an alcove with a cushioned bench. He invites me to sit, and he sits next to me.

I look up at the stars. Oh Devon, I miss you so much.

Charles puts his arms across the back of the bench and asks, "Are you ready for your surprise Fate darling?"

"I guess Charles. What is the surprise?" His arm comes around me and he draws me close, saying, "This…" as he gently but firmly pushes my head away from him and bites my neck. I gasp with the surprise of it, it doesn't hurt after the initial pinch, it feels really nice but I don't want to enjoy it. I feel my life slipping away and I think oh, so he is going to kill me tonight. Then he lifts his mouth from my neck. I watch the stars, they are fuzzy now and I wonder will Devon find me quickly next time? Something wet and hard is shoved in my mouth, blood flows from it. Oh Goddess, he isn't killing me, he's turning me! I clamp down on his wrist and drink deeply, I want to live to see my mate again and I sure as hell don't want to go through being a child again. I feel my body beginning to shift and change. He pulls his arm away as the pain begins. Sweet Lady, this hurts! I wonder how long before it stops? I feel beads of sweat rolling off my forehead as I curl into a ball. Charles rubs my back and I want to snarl at him to stop touching me.

I realize he is talking and I tune in to what he is saying for the distraction, "I'm sorry that you will lose your powers," holy Hera, he thinks this will take away my powers? He goes on to say, "but it is a necessary loss that will allow you to stay with me forever. I know it might upset you now, but one day you will see the good in it. Being a vampire comes with its own abilities. Usually a vampire's special ability will show up within a day or two of the change. While that is when it usually manifests we aren't always aware because sometimes there is no call to use it until much later. But I haven't turned a vampire that didn't end up with a talent. We keep blood in the kitchen here, one of the staff will be happy to fetch as much as you need, there is no need to hunt when humans are so happy to donate it. "

Wow, this guy is so incredibly full of himself. I am not very pleased with it having been Charles that turned me; I wish I was home with Devon. But at least now I am turned, and this dumbass thinks I just lost my powers. I am interested to see if I actually get a new ability from becoming a vampire. Maybe it will help me get the hell out of here. I mean, I know I could air shield myself and stroll out, but that wouldn't keep my family safe. I have to be smart about this, so we all get to live this time.

❧ 24 ❧

DEVON

She has only been gone for a day. I feel so lost without her. I don't even know where to begin; it is all just so overwhelming. I only had her for a few short weeks before he took her from me again. She is alive this time. She is still alive. I will hold tight to that, and maybe we can find her before he kills her.

How will I find her? Where do I start? Billy! Damn my pride or any vampire conventions, Billy is going to train me. Striding through the house, I yell for Billy and hear a response from the direction of the kitchen. Walking in, I see Natasha and Ajah with their heads together over a book and Billy looking at his phone. He looks up when I walk in and says, "The twins should be here in two days. The didn't find Malachi, but they did leave him a message at several villages with people the would seek him out for them."

Nodding, I reply, "That is good news. I have another favor to ask."

"Anything," Billy leans in, "anything at all. How can I help?"

Running my hand across the back of my neck, I take a deep breath. This is still hard to ask, "You know I didn't get any actual training when I was first turned. Or later even," Billy shakes his head yes, "and now I am in a position where I need to be done with being ignorant of so many things in our world. My ignorance has cost me Fate time and again. This time she still lives and I want to make this the last time. Will you train me?" I look down, I don't know what I will do if he says no.

"Of course I will! You could have asked me this at any point since we became friends and I would have helped you. Brothers stick together. You already know a lot more than the average new vamp, training you should occupy just enough time for the twins to arrive. They can teach you a couple things as well, that maybe I could learn too. Ryna is a master at sneak attacks. Being tiny and golden-haired makes people think she would be an excellent target, but then she unleashes hell on them."

Natasha says, "I think I like her already. Maybe she could teach me some dirty tricks."

Billy suddenly looks very uncomfortable with that idea and then Ajah says, "I could teach you how to throw Billy across the room. It would be fun to watch. We could have him help you practice."

Billy is tugging at his t-shirt collar like it is too tight as the girls laugh at him. I realize they have the spell book out and that is what they have been studying so I ask, "I see you have the spell book out, are you looking for something in particular?"

Natasha turns to me, "Well of course we are! We are looking for the right spell to find Fate. There are bunches of spells in here for finding lost people and lost witches. But we need a specific kind. We may end up creating one if we don't find something that fits. I already called Memré and she will be here tomorrow. She hasn't been idle either, her search has focused on Charles and his online presence. Charles Armstrong isn't an unpopular name, unfortunately. She has to sift through them all and find the right one. She may find him before we find her, which could work out as long as he keeps her close to him. If he doesn't, then we will need this as the way to find her. Whatever way works, we will be able to scope out the place and go in with a plan that doesn't get her or us dead."

A tiny ray of hope shines into the well of pain, drowning me slowly. "Thank you."

"Dolt. She's our sister too. We want her back and we are not letting some arrogant asshole take her because… why did he take her? You know him, why is he so hot to fuck you over?"

I explain the whole sorry tale to them, how Charles' mother died and what part he thinks I played in it. "The truth is, his mother died because of his father's gambling debts. I feel certain it was him she was warning him not to go home with, but he won't hear it. So he has been tormenting me ever since. The first thing he was able to do was turn me as part of his revenge. I thought for sure I was done. I didn't think there would be a real life for me after that, and for even longer I truly believed that I would disappear completely if I died. Because I thought that part of becoming a vampire meant you lost your soul. No more reincarnation, no hell, and certainly no heaven. I have been very cautious for a very long time because I thought that if I died, I would never have the chance to see Fate again. Now that I know differently, all I can think is that if I had let myself die at some point, Charles would never have been able to find me or Fate ever again."

Natasha tips her head, "Hmm, well... Not exactly. You all have unfinished business between you. I think Charles will continue to be thrust into your lives until that is resolved. Considering what Fate has gone through, Charles may need to die for him to be out of your lives for good."

I crack my knuckles, "I am good with that plan. I think Charles more than deserves to die at this point. Preferably by my hand, but I am not overly concerned with whose hand it is so long as he dies."

Billy laughs, "Would anyone like to place wagers on who is going to put an end to Charles?"

Ajah lifts her head, "I would. I'll put a twenty on Fate killing him herself after we get there because he is trying to kill us. She walked in there to save us. I think she will take his whole head off if he tries to hurt any of us. Guys, I don't know if you realize it, but we are her family. All of us. I don't think she has ever had a family that treated her half as good as we do, and in a very short time for some of us, we all became really important to her. Just wait, she is going to turn him into confetti."

Natasha nods in agreement, "I can vouch that she never had a family that loved her well. Her parents were always a little stand-offish, and Pru had a shadow of mean running through everything she did with or to Fate. I saw that, and I didn't even know that Pru was mind-raping her all the time. She let go of everything when she was with Charlie because she didn't care about any of it. Except Memré and I. She held on tight to the only two people that ever treated her well, and she has always loved us and would do anything for us. Which is why when Charles had me by the throat and you two cornered by his men, she left with him after extracting a magically bound promise that he would not hurt any of **us**. Not her, she wasn't worried about herself. She doesn't care if she dies so long as we live. Ajah is right. She is going to tear him into kibble."

"I should have found her sooner. I never should have left her in that place."

Natasha shakes her head at me, "Boy. Get over yourself. Has it occurred to you that had you not waited and let her go through these things, find us, and be found by Charles who promptly fell in love with her that she would already be dead? Maybe letting her live apart from you and develop into a whole, fully rounded woman is what has kept her alive this time. For fuck's sake, the audacity. Get trained so you can get rid of Charles if she doesn't and so you can be a better protector to her in general." Natasha goes back to her book with a snort and a "Men!" Under her breath. I look to Billy but he is no help with his hand covering his mouth to keep from laughing as Natasha put me in my place. I ask Billy if he would like to adjourn to my office for scotch and a start to the training. He nods, leans over and kisses Natasha on the forehead, her hand shoots out and gives his a squeeze briefly and he follows me up the stairs.

❄ 25 ❄

NATASHA

It is the wee hours of the morning before I stumble toward my bedroom. I call it mine still, but Billy spends as much time in here as I do. Bits of him linger in the room. His toothbrush in my bathroom, a shirt over the chair. His naked body in my bed right now. Sweet Lady, the man is gorgeous. Beautiful ebony skin, a smile to make the angels weep, and muscles for days. I try to be quiet as I undress, but I hear him roll onto his side for a better view as I undress. "Do you think Memré will find him?"

"I do. She is mad. Big mad. I don't think I have ever seen her this mad, and she helped put her husband in prison after finding sick porn on his computer. She was mad then, but was lucky to have caught things before her husband progressed to abusing children. She kept things quiet, sent her boy to camp so he wouldn't be there to see what happened, and got the sheriff out to her place while the husband was gone. Since it was a shared computer, she could give them permission to dive into it and to put some very specific programs in it that helped them to collect more concrete evidence.

She was calm and collected through the whole thing, handled it with a style and grace that we all have done our best to emulate when we went through our own hard times." Laying down on the bed next to him, I continue, "But when I called her and told her what had happened to Fate, she lost her shit. I swear I heard things hit the wall. She will find him.

And she will show up here ready to go do battle. Fate was the one that stayed with her through it all, not that I went away, just that Fate had more time to spend there and they have known each other their entire lives. Memré will find him and if he is lucky, she won't open up a hole in the earth to droop him in and bury him alive."

"She can do that?"

"Yeah, I think she could. She has some really strong earth magic. I think she could level a few city blocks if she wanted to do it. I don't know that she would break a sweat."

"Damn. I hope she doesn't get mad at me. I do not want to spend twenty years trying to dig myself out of a hole in the ground."

"No, you really don't. I, I have come to a decision. Mostly because I had already been leaning toward doing it anyway, but with what happened to Fate and her requests, well, I decided I definitely want to go through with it."

Billy props his head up with one arm, "What exactly have you decided that you want to go through with?"

"I decided I want to go through with being a vampire. I wanted to run it by you first, because I hope you will be accepting of it and that you would be the one to turn me. However, I am prepared to have one of my friends turn me if you are not ok with it. I do understand if you are not ok with it, and I will be heartbroken if you choose to leave me. I still need to do this. What are your feelings about it?"

"I think it is a great idea. It would honor me to be the one to turn you. I have two questions. The first is why did you think I would be against this? The second is, just how many other vampires do you know?"

I laugh, "I should have known. I try to keep my expectations low. That is not a reflection on you, but on my past. As for how many other vampires I know, well, I haven't stopped to count them. More than a few, but they don't make up the bulk of the people I know. Does that bother you?"

"No. I find you fascinating. Few witches have the wide circle of friends from the various magical communities. Many of the communities are really insular and their members don't welcome those outside their kind of magical. How did you get to be part of so many groups?"

I shrug, "I date. None of it seriously. My grams taught me a lot of things that my mother couldn't or wouldn't and part of that was her open-mindedness. She made sure that any time my mother's stodginess crept in, she was there to smack it out. I asked her why one time. She told me that she had always been really disappointed in my mother for the way she avoided making any waves.

She never misbehaved, never stood up for anything, and stayed perfectly in line with whatever most people were doing. She ignored her magic for the most part because it wasn't accepted with the majority of people. She left Goddess worship for Christianity, she did that with Grams support because Grams would never try to force anyone to be part of any religion. She was the one that first taught my mother about all the various religions. She said Mom's eyes lit up when she heard that Christianity was currently in the top three of religions by the size of its following. She said my Mom immediately asked which one most people here followed and when Grams told her Christianity, she said that she wanted to know more about that one.

Grams quit trying to teach her magic after that. She realized it wasn't the path her daughter wanted for herself, and she couldn't argue with that because it wasn't her life to live. What she could do was make damn sure that any children my mother had knew about magic and all the options before them. So when I was interested she began teaching me and I think a lot of her personality traits became part of mine because I look up to her, then and now.

She always had people of all kinds showing up at her house looking for help with one thing and another. Every time I was there I was meeting humans, shifters of all kinds, vampires, and witches galore. I think there were some demons, really very nice people, and a few fae. The animals were my favorites though. I think a few of them might have been shifters in a bind but, it didn't matter to me because it didn't matter to her. So when I got old enough to date, Grams put the spell on me so I could tell what people were by looking at them. In dating without borders, I made a lot of friends over the years. It gave my community variety and helped me to understand the world better."

"Wow. I think I want to meet your Grams. She sounds amazing."

"She is. So you are really ok with this?"

"I am. It is your choice always, and I believe you wouldn't do a thing like this without thoroughly studying all the angles. I am guessing your Grams gave her approval?"

"Of course she did. I called her after Fate was taken and we talked about it once I stopped crying. She said I should do it because the world needs another good person who can stick around for longer than a minute."

"In that case, when do you want to do it?"

"Now please, I want to be ready when it is time to go after Fate. Plus, I can take advantage of the fact that you are training Devon already. I still plan to train with Ajah, and when the twins arrive, if Ryna is willing to train me in self defense, then I will learn from her too."

"Hmm, sounds like you have this all figured out. Let's see how enjoyable we can make tonight."

❦ 26 ❦

FATE

I didn't expect my first two days as a vampire to be so very strange. I don't know what I did expect, if anything. The night Charles turned me was not the most pleasant. He said that it could have been more pleasant if I was more romantically inclined toward him, but he wouldn't force that kind of intimacy on me. I never would have guessed that as awful as Charles can be, combined with the fact that he has murdered me multiple times, that forcing a woman is where he draws the line. Don't get me wrong, I am not unhappy about that. It is just a facet of Charles I never expected.

He has been a perfect gentleman since he took me, with the exception of turning me without asking my permission.

And the whole kidnapping thing. I don't quite know what to do with that. I mean, he is the definition of a bad guy. Murdering kidnapper. You don't get much worse than that without venturing into things I don't want to think about. He is still filled with ego, but I didn't expect that to change.

I haven't tried to use my phone so far because I wanted to leave it safe in the air bubble. I turned it off on the way here, so it should still have a charge. It is still early morning but I don't sleep a lot without Devon so I am in the library. With my new vampire senses, I can hear so much. Even better, the gift I got is being able to feel where people are in relation to me. There is no one in the house right now, though there are about twenty guards outside in various places. Apparently there was a shipment Charles needed to be there for, wouldn't it be lovely if the feds picked him up?

I set down the book I have been trying to read. I want to call Devon. I am desperate to hear his voice. I don't want to hurt him more by calling, but what if he is feeling the loss as keenly as I am? Fuck it, Imma call him. I walk slowly up the stairs, paying careful attention to where all the warm bodies are, verifying that no one is in the house anywhere. Entering my bedroom I lock the door and throw up an air barrier around the inside of the entire room, just inside that I place another to prevent any sounds from escaping the room. Stepping over to the drawer, I open it and disperse the shield around my phone and purse. Picking up my phone, I leave the drawer hanging open.

Trepidation fills my heart as I turn on the phone and wait for it to load. What if he is mad at me for leaving? Maybe he doesn't care why I left and hates me for leaving with Charles? My battery is still mostly full and my heart in my throat as I pull up Devon's number and hit the call button.

He answers on the first ring, "Fate! Fate, are you ok? Where are you? Love, are you safe? How do we find you?"

"Oh Devon, I just wanted to hear your voice. I miss you so much. I am as safe as I can be. The only thing Charles has done to me beyond the kidnapping is…"

"What Fate? What did he do to you?"

"He, uh, he turned me Devon."

"HE DID WHAT?"

"He turned me. I know you wanted to be the one to do it and you probably want nothing to do with me now, but I just wanted to—"

"Fate. Fate. No. I will always want you. Yes, I wanted to be the one to turn you, but that is because it can be a really erotic thing. He didn't… um… He didn't take advantage of you in that state, did he?"

"What? Oh, no. Surprisingly, no. I wouldn't have thought a murderer would have any morals, but he does have them about that. I have been happily surprised about that. He expects that I will fall in love with him at some point, but he has been delusional for a long time. I can't talk for too long, because I don't know when everyone will be back."

"Are you alone where you're at? Did he leave you unguarded?"

"Ha. No. There are twenty or so guards patrolling the estate. They are all vampires. Your ex-buddy Charles has been a busy boy. I don't know exactly where I am, but I do know I am still in Durham. Did you know Charles is a drug lord? That's where he got all his money from, he took over a drug lord's place in Columbia years ago and has kept the trade going all this time. My vampire door prize is that I can feel where people are for quite a ways away from me. That is how I know where everyone is and that there is no one in the house right now."

"Fate, that is an amazing talent. And it may be really useful. Does he know about your phone? Does he have issues with you having it? Or using it?"

"I don't know, I didn't ask. I have been keeping it turned off and hidden, protected with a shield made of air. He turned me the first night after he took me. My talent came in within minutes. No one has looked for anything in my room. They deliver fresh flowers every morning in here, and I throw them out the window every morning. Pretty sure they are bugged. I put an air shield around my room for this conversation, within the room so that none of the furniture or anything is included, just in case he has anything else bugged in here. I can't leave my phone on, but I can check it at night, if you want to leave me messages."

"I do. And I would love if you would call me when you can. We are working on a way to find you and come get you. This is the end of Charles, when we find him one of us will put a permanent end to him. Natasha is working on a spell to find you, Ajah is helping her. The twins, Seamus and Ryna, are on their way. Memré is working to find Charles online, Natasha says she is big mad. Mad in a way that she has never seen, including when she put her husband in prison?"

"Oh my. Durham might end up with a new fault line… Shit. Devon, they are pulling into the driveway. I have to go. I love you so much. Don't give up on me, I am coming back to you as soon as I figure out a way to do it without putting you all in danger."

"Don't worry Fate. I love you, and I will be coming for you soon. Just sit tight."

"No Devon, just be patient. I will come back to you."

"Ok love, we'll wait for you then. I love you."

"I love you."

DEVON

I run downstairs to the kitchen; it seems to be the gathering place and where everyone is usually working now. I burst in and everyone looks up at me; Natasha, Billy, Ajah, Steve, Owen, John, Brad, Maria and her two helpers. "Fate called me!"

There is a clamor as everyone wants to know if Fate is ok and do I know where she is and are we leaving now? I hold up my hands and everyone quiets down, "Yes, she is ok. No, I don't know exactly where she is beyond Durham. She is still in Durham. No, we can't leave to go get her yet, it is a little more complicated than that. Charles is a drug lord. Natasha, you may want to pass that on to Memré. He started out in Columbia."

Natasha snatches her phone up saying, "On it."

"Also, Charles turned her already. So she is a little bit safer, sort of. She doesn't have any training because Charles doesn't do that. Fate also said she wants us to wait for her to come back to us when she figures out how to do it safely."

Billy raises an eyebrow, "Are you going to do that?"

I smile for the first time in days, "Not a chance."

Author's Note

REVIEWS REALLY HELP OTHER PEOPLE DECIDE WHETHER OR not to read a book. If you feel a way about this book, I would sincerely appreciate a review.

ABOUT THE AUTHOR

Rhiannon writes steamy paranormal romance. She is an avid reader of many authors in a variety of genre though she tends more toward paranormal.

She has three former pound puppies that she dotes on and three daughters that she adores.

Rhiannon has lived in multiple states though she is currently residing in North Carolina. Wandering, witching, and reading with her puppies and husband are what she does when she isn't writing.

To learn about what is happening in Rhiannon's world and get loads of pupper cuteness, sign up for the by using the QR code below to visit my website.

Mercy of the Vampire King

Shame of the Vampire King

Pursuit of the Vampire King

Prey of the Vampire King

Reign of the Vampire King

Coming Soon

Love and Vampires Series

Olivia's Fall

Olivia's Prison

Olivia's Flight

Olivia's Family

Warriors of the Old Gods

A Dream of Blood

A Dream of Wolves

A Dream of Stone

A Dream of Ravens

A Dream of Bones